MURDER ON ARTHUR'S SEAT

DI MCKENZIE BOOK 1

ANNA-MARIE MORGAN

For Jean, with love

ALSO BY ANNA-MARIE MORGAN

The DI Giles Series (21 books)

Book 1 - Death Master

Book 2 - You Will Die

Book 3 - Total Wipeout

Book 4 - Deep Cut

Book 5 - The Pusher

Book 6 - Gone

Book 7 - Bone Dancer

Book 8 - Blood Lost

Book 9 - Angel of Death

Book 10 - Death in the Air

Book 11 - Death in the Mist

Book 12 - Death under Hypnosis

Book 13 - Fatal Turn

Book 14 - The Edinburgh Murders

Book 15 - A Picture of Murder

Book 16 - The Wilderness Murders

Book 17 - The Bunker Murders

Book 18 - The Garthmyl Murders

Book 19 - The Signature

Book 20 - The Incendiary Murders

Book 21 - The Park Murders

1

TAKEN

Gordon stood at the bar of the Last Drop, a tavern in Edinburgh's Old Town, feeling relaxed.

The pub was his sort of place; a respite from the outside world where he could relax amid historic walls and modern-day comfort, enjoying a traditional ale or a craft beer with friends. Dark wooden tables and high-backed chairs invited patrons to settle in for a leisurely drink or a hearty meal. Adorned with old photographs and memorabilia, the walls offered a glimpse into Edinburgh's past and the pub's rich history. Dim lighting provided the escape from reality he craved, while the mixed scent of traditional Scottish dishes such as haggis, neeps, and tatties or fish and chips filtered from the restaurant, reminding him of a childhood at his grandparent's croft. The tavern's ambience was homely and inviting; a haven where anxieties melted away and conversation thrived, even if it deteriorated into a drunken blether by the end of the night.

He looked across at Shania, her long blonde hair in a single plait like fancy French bread. Gordon thought it odd she spent her one night off drinking at her workplace. But he was glad she did. He preferred her on this side of the bar. There were no barriers between them. She had her back to him, allowing his gaze to wander her elegant neck as he agonised over asking her out, something he wanted do before starting a marine biology course at Edinburgh University in the autumn. Language was easy until butter-flies took over and words became an incomprehensible mess. At least, they did for him.

It was his round and, as he handed over two crisp banknotes to the bartender, he signalled to his friends for help to get the drinks to their table.

After a short debate, Gordon's best mate was the chosen helper. Jock, dark-haired and small-boned, was almost a foot shorter than his friend. It brought out the protective instinct in Goose. The two of them, several packs of nuts between their teeth, carried six pints and a whiskey-coke over to the others.

"So, are you going to do it, then?" Jock asked, as they plonked the pints in front of thirsty friends.

"I don't know... I want to, it's just..."

"Just what? Look at her. She's over there waiting."

Gordon snuck another glance. "No, she's not... She's not even looking."

"Aye, but she was a wee while earlier. You know it. Come on, it's now or never. You'll be too busy to bother once your course starts. You'll miss your chance if you don't try now. Old golden chops over there will get to her first," Jock gestured to their fair-haired, handsome friend, Ben. Broad, with a shirt that stressed gym-going biceps, Ben was the one with a reputation for the girls.

Gordon grimaced. "Och, thanks, mate... That's all I need. Jings, he better not go over there, eh?"

"Well, go do it then." Jock gestured again with his head. "Talk to her."

"Aye, I'll need a smoke first. I need to work up to it."

"Well, don't leave it too long, eh?"

Gordon pulled a pack of cigarettes from his pocket and headed through the door onto the street. Heart pumping hard, it took three attempts to light one. Trembling hands made a mess of the matches. "Look at the state of me," he said aloud. "She'll not want to see me if I'm shaking like this."

The screech of brakes and tyres scraping along the road shook him out of his reverie. He had no time to react.

Three men in balaclavas and black clothing clambered out of a dark SUV with tinted windows. They grabbed Gordon while his mouth fell open, forcing a cloth bag over his head.

As the SUV sped away, the virgin cigarette burned red in the gutter where it had fallen.

INSIDE THE PUB, Jock checked his watch. Gordon had been gone for over twenty minutes. That wasn't like him. There was a serious frost developing outside, and Goose wasn't one to be standing out in the cold for long. In fact, Gordon's nickname came about because of the pimpled flesh he broke out in at the mere mention of chill weather.

It didn't take this long to drum up the courage to speak to a lassie. Joch strode to the door of the pub to check on his friend.

As cold air stung his cheeks, he peered both ways along the street. His mate was nowhere to be seen. "Gordon?" he called. "Goose?" Frowning, he returned to their friends.

"Where's Gord?" Mikey Murray asked, eyebrows raised.

Joch shrugged. "He said he was going for a smoke, but I can't find him. He's not outside, I looked."

"I'll check the bog. I need to go, anyway." Mikey got up. "He's probably making himself pretty for Shania over there..."

Joch laughed, but his eyes didn't crease. Something was up. He knew it.

SATURDAY MORNING, and Grant McKenzie was home with his family in one of The Grange's smaller Victorian properties, in the leafy suburbs south of Edinburgh city centre. All were still in their pyjamas.

The DI panted after running round the lounge as an aeroplane and carrying six-year-old Craig on his back. Four-year-old Martha rode on his leg, both her tiny feet on one of his.

Ten-year-old Davie gave them a stern look and a sigh. Considering himself far too old for such games, he pulled a face, unable to hear the cartoon he was watching.

"I'm hungry," Craig complained as his dad dropped him onto the carpet.

"Me too." Martha rubbed her eyes. "And I'm thirsty."

"Aye, well, your mammy will have breakfast on the table in a few minutes. Why don't you two go wash your hands and face? By the time you finish, your food will be ready."

As the younger children left to do as he asked, the phone rang.

His sister was on the other end, her words delivered in breathless, clipped sentences.

"Gordon is missing... He's vanished, Grant. My boy didn't come home last night and his friends can't find him."

"Woah, Davina, slow down, hen. What do you mean his friends can't find him? He's a young lad. Maybe he stayed with a lassie?"

"You don't understand. He went outside to smoke, and didn't come back."

"What, at your house?"

"No, no, the pub. He was with friends at the Last Drop. They said he popped outside for a smoke, and never came back. Jock and the others looked for him everywhere. They said he vanished into thin air. I'm scared. Something's wrong."

The DI's heart pumped hard in his chest. He cleared his throat, keeping his voice calm and measured. "Look, sis, try not to worry. I'll get searching for him right away. Have you called the station?"

"Yes, I did, but they said they couldn't do anything until he's been missing for at least twenty-four hours."

"I'll handle it. Don't worry. I'll be there soon," Grant assured her, hanging up the phone. He headed for the kitchen to let his wife, Jane, know he had to leave.

2

WORRIED KIN

The Last Drop tavern in Grassmarket was a place historically known as the site of public executions; the last drop referring to the ultimate sip of liquor taken by those souls condemned to death.

The area was merely a short walk from the Royal Mile and Edinburgh Castle. Filled with pubs, restaurants, and shops, it was popular with both locals and tourists.

Jock stood outside of the Last Drop, his face etched with worry. "Thank God you're here, Mr McKenzie." His voice trembled. "Gordon went outside for a smoke last night and never came back. We searched everywhere, but there was no sign of him. I came down here this morning to see if I could see him about. But, I've been up and down this street, and spoken to the landlord here. Nobody knows anything. Nobody saw anything. I wouldn't feel so bad, except I spoke to a couple last night who were drinking at a table near the door. They said they heard the screeching of tyres at one point, but couldn't be sure of the time. They were obviously drunk." He ran both hands through his hair. "It could have been about the time Goose went out for a smoke but, if there was a car out there, it had gone by the time I went looking for him. I searched for a while, and then I rang his mum to see if he had gone back home. But she said he hadn't returned. What do we do?"

"Did the couple you spoke to see a vehicle?"

"No, and when I questioned them again, they didn't know what I was talking about."

"Not the best witnesses, then."

Jock shook his head. "They were too busy drinking. Like I said, they had forgotten all about it when I spoke to them a second time."

Grant put a hand on the anxious lad's shoulder. "Did you see him talking to a girl last night? Someone with a jealous boyfriend? Anybody else? Somebody he wouldn't normally speak to? Anyone dodgy?"

"Gordon was with us. We hadn't been here long. I helped him carry drinks back to the lads, and he said he was going for a smoke. I didn't see him speak to anyone else apart from the barman to order our beers."

"Can you think of anyone who might have had a grudge or a reason to harm him?"

Jock thought for a moment. "Well, there was this guy he had an argument with a few nights back. It got pretty heated, but I don't know if that has anything to do with this."

"Who was the guy?"

He shrugged. "I don't know. We had come out of a club, and a lad about our age bumped into Goose, almost knocking him over. He didn't apologise, and Gordon asked him to look where he was going. They exchanged words, but it didn't come to blows. At one point, I thought it would. But Gordon brushed himself down, and we moved on. And that was that."

"Had you seen the guy before?"

He shook his head. "I didn't recognise him."

"We'll need a description. Can you pop by Leith station later?"

"Sure." Jock hung his head. "It's not much though, eh?"

The DI put an arm on his shoulder. "Look, it's a lead. If Goose doesn't turn up, I'll want to know everything about that argument, and anything else you can tell me, to help us find him. But right now, I think you should get yourself off home. Likely, Gordon will show up today. If he doesn't? Well... we'll cross that bridge when we come to it."

GRANT'S SISTER DAVINA STRACHAN, a watercolour artist, lived in a three-bedroom Victorian house on a tree-lined street in Morningside, to the southwest of Edinburgh city centre. A reasonably affluent area, it was popular with both childless professionals and families looking for a quiet life away from the bustling city.

She and her husband Jim had lived there since they were married. Davina had given birth to their daughter Mona in a bedroom of the property fifteen years before, when Gordon was six, and had only recently celebrated her forty-third birthday.

She opened the door before Grant reached it. Dressed in jeans and a roll-neck jumper, she looked dehydrated; her face lined with concern. Her red hair hung ragged from the anxious hand-combing she had done for the last several hours. "Thank God you're here..." She stepped back for him to enter. "Jim's gone to look for Gordon. He left a couple of hours ago."

"Have you heard anything?" The DI pulled her into his

arms for a reassuring hug. He was nearly a foot taller than she, which was just as well. He hadn't shaved in a week, and didn't enjoy inflicting stubble-burn on a woman unnecessarily. His beard would be soft soon enough.

Davina leaned her head on his shoulder. "Thank you for coming."

"I popped by the Last Drop on the way here." His deep voice vibrated her hair. "I spoke to Jock... The boy searched all of Grassmarket before I got there. I told him to go home for something to eat and drink. He looked worn out."

"He's a good lad." She nodded, looking up at her brother's eyes; her own, wide and earnest. "This is so unlike Gordon. Do you think he is all right?"

Grant thought of what Jock had said about the unknown man crashing into his nephew days before. "I'm sure he is... And we will find him, sis." He sounded more certain than he felt, but Davina's shoulders were less tense as she pulled away.

"Would you like a brew before you go?" She asked, her blue eyes on the window.

He checked his watch, thinking of his children and the abandoned playtime of which there was always so precious little. But it was clear his sister did not want to be alone again, yet. He closed his eyes. "Sure... I'll have a swift cuppa with you, and then I best get on. When Jim gets back, phone the local hospitals. And, if we still haven't found Gordon, contact the station again. See if you can complete a missing person's form ready for submission if he hasn't turned up by tonight." He saw the fear in her watery blue eyes. "He will turn up, sis... Trust in that. We will find him."

3

SHANIA MCINNES

The DI's heart lay heavy in his chest as he climbed the stairs in Leith station. The dark stone facade, in the city's north, held more foreboding for him this morning. Gordon had not made contact, and had neither accessed his bank account nor used his phone or social media. Someone had switched off his mobile, or it had died, minutes after he left his friends for a smoke outside of the Last Drop, the last time the phone pinged a local cell tower. None of this boded well.

Inside the office, forty-two-year-old DC Graham Dalgliesh sat typing a report, looking smart in an expensive shirt and tie, his short sandy hair recently cut. "Hey," he called out to the DI, whose own shirt had not been ironed that morning.

McKenzie straightened his tie, and ran a hand through short dark hair in need of a trim before hanging his overcoat next to the door, and plonking a briefcase on his desk. "Hey, yourself..." He sighed. "It's been a bit of a weekend..."

Dalgliesh pushed his chair away from the desk with his feet, swivelling around to face the latecomer. "What happened?" His eyes narrowed with concern. "Are you okay?"

McKenzie sighed. "My nephew, Gordon, is missing. He disappeared from outside of the Last Drop on Friday night, and there's been no contact from him since. My sister is frantic, and I have a bad feeling about this."

"Christ!" Dalgleish frowned. "He got a girlfriend?"

The DI shook his head.

"He'll turn up though, eh? I mean, he wouldn't be the first laddie to go off with a lass he just met..."

"Aye, but he's not contacted anyone, and that's not like him, Graham. It's not like him at all."

"Did he get in with the wrong crowd?"

Grant shook his head. "He's got a good bunch of friends. His bestie spent all of Saturday looking for him. He said Goose popped outside for a smoke, and didn't come back."

DS Susan Robertson entered with DC Helen McAllister, deep in conversation about their respective weekends.

"Aye, in your own time, you two, eh?" Dalgleish grinned at them before turning his attention back to the DI.

Grant nodded in greeting to the two women as they pulled faces back at Dalgleish. He returned to the conversation. "I'll speak with the DCI. Ask him if we can look into it."

Graham frowned. "Aye, good luck with that... I doubt Rob will let us near it just now. I know it's your nephew and all, but there's nothing to say this is anything serious. Not yet, anyway... And he might think you're too close to the case. You know what he's like. He does everything by the book... You know it. "

"Goose got into an altercation last week. Some guy rammed into him in the street. They exchanged words. It got quite heated, apparently. That is not like Goose. He's usually pretty easygoing."

"You think the argument had something to do with his disappearance?"

Grant shrugged. "Maybe?"

"Aye, well, there's no harm in asking then. Go for it. I'll back you up."

"Thanks." He turned to the two women. "Good morning, Sue... Helen."

"Good morning, sir. You're looking a tad serious there?" DS Susan Robertson walked over to them, straightening her blouse and hand-combing her brunette bob. "What's wrong?"

DC Helen McAllister watched from her desk, putting a brush through her own wind-blown ash-blonde locks.

"His nephew's done a runner." Dalgleish leaned back in his chair.

"He's not done a runner." Grant sighed, tossing his head at the DC. "Don't listen to him... Gordon disappeared on Friday night while he was smoking outside of the Last Drop. He's not been heard from since, and he hasn't used his bank card or mobile phone."

"Jeezo..." Robertson frowned. "Have you contacted the hospitals? What have uniform said? Is he official, yet?"

McKenzie nodded. "He's been officially missing for fifty-six hours."

"If he intended disappearing, where would he have gone? What's he into? Could it be a girl?"

"According to his best friend, Jock, Gordon quite likes a lass called Shania McInnes."

"Aye, well, maybe he's with her? Have you contacted her?"

Grant shook his head. "Jock said she was still at the pub an hour after my nephew vanished. Goose had not even asked her out. He was working up to it, apparently. He was going to do it after his smoke. That's what makes this more worrying."

"Cold feet can make folk do odd things." Dalgleish scratched his chin. "Maybe he ran because his mates were pressuring him to talk to her?"

"Sure, I could buy that..." The DI sighed. "But if that was the case, he would have turned up by now. He'd have gone home to bed and been with his family the next day."

Helen McAllister joined them from behind her desk. "I agree. If it was nerves about asking a girl out, he would be home by now. And he'd have been on his phone or social media apologising to his friends."

"So, what are you going to do? Are we looking into it?" Dalgleish cocked his head.

"Aye, I want to. I'll speak to Sinclair," Grant nodded, referring to their DCI. "If he doesn't think I'm too close..."

"Well, he's in his office." Dalgleish nodded towards the DCI's door. "He was in early this morning."

"Aye, okay. Wish me luck."

ROB SINCLAIR'S voice boomed from the other side of the door.

"Come in."

McKenzie pushed it open.

"Ah, Grant, good morning."

"Good morning, sir." The DI cleared his throat.

"What's the matter? You look worried." The forty-nine-year-old DCI rocked back in his chair.

McKenzie couldn't help his gaze falling on Sinclair's shirt-front and emerging pot-belly. He shifted his attention to his superior's face, searching for eyes under the glare from his glasses. "I wanted to speak with you about my nephew, Gordon Strachan... He's missing and it's not like him."

"I'm sorry to hear that. What happened?" Sinclair returned his chair to an upright position, smoothing the sparse hair on the top of his head, forehead creased with concern.

"He was out with friends. He went for a smoke and didn't come back. No-one has heard from him since, and he hasn't accessed his bank account or social media. My sister has tried phoning and messaging him, to no avail. His phone has been off, and it hasn't pinged a cell tower since he went outside of the Last Drop in Grassmarket." McKenzie sighed. "My sister, Davina, is beside herself. Her husband, Jim, was out all day yesterday looking for him."

"That doesn't sound good." Sinclair pursed his lips.

McKenzie nodded. "No, it doesn't. Gordon's a responsible lad, and he wouldn't just disappear like this. I think something has happened to him. Something bad."

Sinclair leaned forward, his fingers steepled beneath his chin. "Have you spoken with uniform? Maybe he got into trouble and they picked him up?"

"I spoke to the duty sergeant. There's no record of his being picked up and no incidents involving him. His friends have been searching for him all weekend too, with no luck."

"Alright, I understand your concern. I'll authorise a missing person investigation. You and your team can look into it, but I want regular updates. And keep me informed of significant developments."

"Thank you, sir. I appreciate it." McKenzie nodded, relieved Sinclair was taking it seriously.

"You're his uncle, and I understand you want to be

involved. But make sure you remain objective. I'll reassess when we have more information."

"Of course... My team will keep me on track."

Sinclair leaned back in his chair. "Right... well, you best get on. Keep it professional and keep me in the loop."

"Aye, will do."

McKenzie rejoined his team, relieved he could take the case but worried about the responsibility. His sister might not forgive him if he messed up.

BACK IN THE MAIN OFFICE, he gathered DS Robertson and DC McAllister to his desk. "Listen... We're investigating Gordon's disappearance. I want all hands on deck. Susan, I need you to coordinate with uniform and gather any information they have. Check again with hospitals in case he was picked up overnight. Helen, please start digging into Gordon's background; his friends, his activities. Let's find out what he's been into recently, and whether we can link any of it to his disappearance."

The two women strode to their desks and got to work.

McKenzie continued. "Graham, can you gather all CCTV from around the Last Drop and Grassmarket? Someone may have captured what happened or have footage of potential witnesses."

"Aye, got it," Dalgliesh answered, picking up the phone. "What are you going to do?"

"I'm going to visit my sister again; look at Gordon's room, and find out if he has contacted either her or Jock. I want to know more about this Shania McInnes."

ACCORDING to Gordon's best friend Jock Munro, twenty-year-old Shania McInnes was often to be found in the Last Drop either drinking with friends or serving customers.

Grant decided he would start there, after his sister confirmed her son had still not made contact.

He found the girl sitting behind the bar during a quiet period; gazing through the window to the street, where a quiet drizzle greased the pavement running alongside the road. McKenzie could see why Gordon felt drawn to her. She had a fragile, unearthly quality. With round, soulful, grey eyes and a diminutive, svelte figure, she was like a small bird. To approach was to fear her taking flight. "Miss McInnes? Shania McInnes?" he asked, tilting his head to appear less threatening since she was on her own.

She jumped out of her daydream, eyes wide, rising as though standing to attention. She pushed stray strands of corn-blonde hair behind her ears.

Was it that obvious he was the police? Must be the long black overcoat. His wife joked that wearing it made him look like a spook from MI5. He held up his ID. "DI Grant McKenzie, I'm here to ask you about a missing person, last seen in this bar on Saturday night."

Her eyes narrowed, a confused look crossing her face. "Who?"

"A lad named Gordon Strachan, about your age... Maybe a year or two older."

"Gordon..." She frowned. "The name rings a bell... I cannae put a face to it, though, I'm afraid."

"Were you working last Saturday?"

"No, I wasn't. I was here, right enough... I was drinking with some friends. I suppose you think that odd, eh? Drinking with my pals in the place where I work?"

He shrugged. "I hadn't thought about it, but yes... I

suppose it is a little odd. Most people can't wait to get away from the workplace when they socialise."

"Aye well, I like the old place. I mean, I don't always drink here. But sometimes I do."

"Right..." He rubbed his chin, smoothing his developing beard. "His nickname is Goose. He went for a smoke about ten-fifteen on Saturday night, and didn't come back. No-one has seen or heard from him since. His best friend is Jock Munro."

"Jock? Oh, I know him. Maybe I saw his friend?" She scratched her head. "What was he wearing?"

"A thick, blue-check lumberjack shirt and jeans," he answered without checking his notes. He didn't need to. "He has red hair and green eyes... and freckles over his nose. Think Ed Sheeran, and you won't be far wrong."

"That gives me an image..." She thought about it for a moment, her grey eyes on the floor. "I don't recall seeing anyone like that." She sighed, bringing her gaze back to the detective. "Sorry..."

Grant thought he caught a flicker in those eyes. But she quickly suppressed it. "You're sure you don't remember him?" His forehead furrowed. Why would she lie to him? "You would tell me?"

She shrugged, flicking her head. "I would. I told you, I don't know him."

"Who are you afraid of?"

"No-one."

"You sure about that?"

She swallowed. "Yes."

"Was there any trouble in here that night?"

"Trouble?" She shook her head, tense shoulders relaxing. "No, it was all pretty civil. I didn't have to call the police once."

"Did you notice anything off? Something that didn't seem right?"

"No, nothing."

He paused, pressing his lips together, sure Shania was hiding something. He made a mental note to investigate it further, though now was not the right time. Let her think about it for a while. "All right... Well, thanks. Is it okay for us to put a flier in your window?"

"Aye, I don't see why not. You care about him, eh? Is he a relation?"

His shoulders stiffened. "Why do you ask that?"

She shrugged. "I sense things about people... Guess it comes with the job. I feel people's emotions, you ken? You seem like you know him, is all."

"Will you let us know if he comes in?" He pushed his card across the table towards her. "We'd really appreciate it."

"Of course." She said, without smiling. "I'll call you."

As HE LEFT the tavern for the walk to his car, he had the feeling those soulful grey eyes were on his back. He gave himself a mental shake, lifting his collar against the dreich and drizzle.

4

THE MEN IN BLACK

"Boss..." DC Graham Dalgliesh ran a hand through his sandy hair before tucking his shirt in. He wasn't one for the unkempt look, but scouring CCTV footage for twelve hours with nary a break would make anyone look crumpled.

"Aye, what have got for me?" McKenzie took off his suit jacket, hanging it over the back of his chair.

"I've been through the CCTV from every camera around the Last Drop."

"And?"

"You need to come see this..." Dalgliesh's face darkened. "I'm sorry, Grant... You will not like it." He sighed. "They took Gordon from outside of the tavern."

"Who did?" McKenzie frowned. "So the drunken witnesses were correct?"

"Aye... A group of men pulled up in what looks like a black SUV. It was over in moments. Three of them, in balaclavas."

"Och, Christ!" McKenzie crossed to Dalgliesh's desk,

joined by Helen and Susan, who also wanted to see the footage.

McKenzie, his heart pounding, leaned closer to the screen while the kidnapping played out before them. Grainy black and white images showed the dimly lit street outside the Last Drop tavern. His nephew, Gordon, appeared from inside, his face momentarily illuminated as he lit a cigarette.

McKenzie clenched his fists.

The black SUV came in fast; three figures clad in dark clothing and balaclavas jumped out.

The team watched, incredulous at the swift and coordinated nature of the abduction. In a matter of seconds, the abductors surrounded Gordon and dragged him into the waiting vehicle with a bag over his head. As the door slammed shut, the SUV sped away. Grant's nephew had stood no chance.

"Twenty-five seconds," Helen observed.

Susan cursed.

McKenzie's mind raced, filled with anger, worry, and confusion. He replayed the scene in his head. The images etched into his memory. "We'll need extra support," he said, finally. "I'll ask Sinclair. It looks like organised crime."

"That's what I thought." Dalgleish nodded. "And Helen is right. It was all over in less than thirty seconds. Someone thoroughly planned this. They knew exactly what they were doing, and how to execute it without being stopped."

"Goose wouldn't have known what hit him."

Graham continued. "I've enhanced the footage as best as I can. Look at this... I'll zoom in here."

He honed in on one of the balaclava-clad figures. McKenzie's jaw clenched as he looked for distinguishing features. A pulse throbbed in his temples. "Is that a scar? At the corner of his left eye, can you see that?"

"I see it," Susan Robertson affirmed. "That should help."

"We've got to find him," McKenzie growled, his voice low. "We need to locate that damned SUV; find out who those bastards are."

Helen nodded. "I'll contact traffic division and get them to scour footage from every camera in that part of the city for the route the SUV took. They must be on other cameras. We should be able to map at least part of their route."

Susan chimed in, her voice steady. "Did you run a check on the plates, Graham?"

"That's the other thing..." Dalgleish sat on the edge of his desk, hands in his pockets. "The registration plates were false. Tracing their origins will be difficult and may not provide us with an address in the short term."

McKenzie turned back to the screen. "Aye well, let's pull every resource we can. I can't rest until we find Gordon and get him home. Somehow, I've got to tell my sister that thugs abducted her twenty-one-year-old son, my nephew, on a night out. Christ, how will I do that?"

"I don't envy you..." DS Robertson scratched her head. "We should call a press conference. We'll need the public's help. There will have been others who saw that vehicle leave, screeching away in the night. It's something they would remember. Someone may have recognised the group, or may know something of what was going down."

"Agreed." McKenzie nodded. "I'll call one for this afternoon. The sooner we get a lead on this bunch, the better. Check the database for anyone listed as having a scar at the corner of their left eye."

∿

GRANT WALKED TO HIS CAR, steps and heart heavy; sick to his stomach. His insides felt hollowed out. His muscles were so taught they ached. The dark news he must deliver weighed on him as if the air itself had become dense; suffocating. His mind raced, trying to find the right words; the best way to tell his sister and her daughter what had happened to Gordon.

He could have phoned Davina, but didn't want to impart the news without being there to comfort her. No, this was best served in person, and with hugs and words of reassurance; delivered with a confidence he might not be feeling. He would stay until Jim got home from work. Mona, Gordon's fifteen-year-old sister, would be home from school any minute. This would be tough on both mum and daughter. But, perhaps, they could provide some nugget or suggestion about who might have taken Goose, and why.

The drive to his sister's Georgian home in Morningside felt longer than usual. Fingers tapped nervously on the steering wheel, his thoughts a whirlwind of uncertainty. He parked the car and took a deep breath, steadying himself before stepping out and walking to the front door.

As he knocked, it swung open, revealing his sister. Her brow furrowed as she looked at her brother's troubled face. "Grant, what is it? Have you found him?"

He forced a smile that didn't reach his eyes. "Can I come in, sis? We need to talk."

She stepped aside, allowing him to enter. The interior of the house, usually cosy and familiar, felt like a chamber of foreboding. Mona's school bag lay spilling contents onto the couch, a stark metaphor for the young girl's world which was about to be turned upside down.

As he considered this, the lounge door swung open, and in walked Goose's sister. She stopped short upon seeing her uncle in their house during the workday, a worried look on her face. "Uncle Grant? Have you found him?"

He cleared his throat, catching a few extra moments to find the right words. "Mona, I need you and your mum to sit down. There's something... something I need to tell you."

"What's happened?" Davina sat on the couch. Her worried gaze locked with her brothers.

He hesitated, shifting his eyes between his sister and her daughter, knowing the impact his words would have. "It's about Gordon," he began, his voice low and sombre. "Three masked men abducted him in a black SUV. They took him from outside of the Last Drop tavern when he went for a smoke."

Davina gasped, a hand flying to her mouth, her eyes wide with shock. "Kidnapped? But... but why? Who would want to do that to Goose?"

Grant's heart ached at his sister's distress. He wished he had answers, but all he could offer were questions. "We don't know, yet. There is footage from several CCTV systems, but the abductors wore face masks, and the SUV plates were false. We're still trying to figure out who the men are and why they took him."

Mona stared motionless, her face drained of colour; eyes brimming with tears. "Is he going to be okay?"

The DI's own eyes clouded over as he placed a comforting hand on his niece's shoulder. "We're doing everything we can to find him, Mona. We are throwing everything at the case. This is our bread and butter, and we won't stop until we have him back. I can promise you that."

Davina wiped away a tear, her voice shaky. "I have to do something... I can't just sit here."

Grant nodded "I know how you feel, sis. But you must leave the searching to us. This gang is likely dangerous. We won't sit idle, you know that. I need you to stay strong... All of you. There is something you can do for Gordon, though. You must try to remember the things he said recently. The things he did, places he visited, and the people he met. No matter how insignificant they might have seemed, there could be clues within his actions to what happened. Have a think about it for me, and let us know if you remember anything that could help piece together who they are and why they abducted him. I'd like to go through his room, too, if that's okay with you?"

His sister nodded. "Of course... whatever you need."

THE STAIRS COMPLAINED as he took them two at a time to Gordon's room at the end of the landing. Each creak increased his apprehension. Reaching the door, he found it ajar, as though the room was inviting him in.

The DI donned latex gloves before entering, the snap of the material punctuating the air. The room felt suspended in time, frozen since its occupant's absence. Grant knew within its walls might lie the clues to his nephew's whereabouts. The smallest detail, the seemingly inconsequential, might be the key to why he was taken.

Grant's eyes swept across the room, taking in the neatly made bed, scattered books on the desk, and posters of marine life that adorned the walls. These were the fragments of Gordon's world, the pieces that held his essence. To know the perpetrators, you had to know the victim. And though he felt he understood his nephew, it was nigh-on impossible to know everything about someone. And a young person's life could change so fast. The wrong crowd or situation could upend everything in a heartbeat.

Having said that, Gordon was an intelligent twenty-one-year-old. He was due to begin a marine biology course at Edinburgh University the following year, after taking three years out after school to go travelling. He wasn't really the sort to get in with the wrong crowd, and there had been no indications of substance abuse.

The DI moved with purpose, methodically examining the space. Gloved fingers brushed over books, their titles a glimpse into Gordon's interests and intellect. Marine ecology and conservation were the subjects that fuelled his nephew's passion. Grant's heart ached at the thought of the potential that lay within this young man, a future that might now be uncertain.

As he sifted through belongings, memories of their shared moments occupied his mind: family gatherings, outings to the coast, and the times when he himself had imparted life lessons to Goose during impromptu babysitting, or a family visit. But a person could bury untold secrets in the depths of their existence. Grant knew that even with the bond they shared, there would be facets of his nephew's life of which he was unaware.

A photograph caught his attention, nestled among the books. It was a picture of Gordon and his friends, their smiles frozen in a moment of camaraderie. Grant studied the faces, wondering if there was more to these friendships than met the eye. He recognised Jock Munro, Goose's best friend, and Mikey Murray, another friend. They were good lads, and unlikely to be the cause of what happened.

Grant's mind wandered back to the nightmarish reality of the masked men and the SUV. Perhaps Gordon's abduction was simply a case of being in the wrong place at the wrong time. Maybe the kidnapping had been a case of mistaken identity. In which case, Goose would turn up soon, frightened, disorientated, but none the worse for wear. Unfortunately, this was unlikely. The world was increasingly a place where people smuggling, drug trafficking, and sex trafficking were all too common. These scenarios were hard to think about when searching for a loved one. But he was a police officer heading up a major investigation team. For him, there was no choice. He had to consider such things.

His gloved fingers paused over a journal on the desk, its pages filled with Gordon's thoughts, dreams, and observations. With gentle reverence, the DI opened it, his eyes scanning words which had captured the young man's journey. There were musings about the ocean, expressions of wonder at the creatures beneath its surface, and personal reflections hinting at Gordon's hopes and dreams.

As his gaze wandered along words written in fountain pen, he felt a renewed determination. This book that held his nephew's essence wanted the answers as much as the rest of them.

He left the room, softly closing the door.

5

BODY ON ARTHUR'S SEAT

McKenzie straightened his tie and tamed his hair with a wet hand, staring in the mirror at the dark shadows under his eyes. He looked ten years older.

DC Dalgleish joined him in the toilets. "They're waiting for you, sir... The room is full," he said, referring to the journalists and hacks waiting in the conference room for news.

McKenzie rolled his sleeves down, buttoning them before putting on his suit jacket as though donning armour. He filled his lungs. "Right, Graham, let's do this."

The room rattled with cameras, microphones, and the excited chatter of reporters, their tone changing from bored to expectant as the detectives entered. The noise level dropped tens of decibels.

McKenzie tapped his microphone, flanked by Dalgleish on one side, and DS Susan Robertson on the other. "Er, hello. Thank you, everyone, for coming." The speakers gave a high-pitched whistle, and the DI moved a few inches further from the microphone before outlining what they knew, or what he could tell the waiting crowd of what they knew.

"Is it true that they have found Gordon Strachan's body?" shouted a male journalist near the back of the room.

McKenzie stopped in his tracks, heart thumping in his chest. "I'm sorry. What did you say?" His forehead furrowed as he focussed on the reporter.

"I was just saying, I heard they found a body up on Arthur's Seat about half an hour ago. I'm sorry, I thought you knew?"

The DI looked first at Susan Robertson, and then at Graham Dalgleish.

Susan shook her head.

Dalgleish shrugged.

"Where did you get this information?" McKenzie asked the reporter, before leaning closer to Dalgleish to request he go talk to the uniformed inspector downstairs and find out what the hell was going on.

"We heard it on the way here," the newsman continued.

Grant cleared his throat, moving his hands underneath the lectern to hide the shaking. "We're checking the veracity of your information. Meanwhile, and supposing what you heard is correct, what makes you think it was Gordon?"

"The dead man's clothing matches those the Strachan lad was last seen wearing."

The DI did his best to hide it his sinking heart from the reporters, but he wanted to run all the way to Arthur's Seat, to see for himself. "If that is true, then it is a sad day indeed. We'll close this press conference for now and reconvene tomorrow when we know more. DS Susan Robertson will give you all fliers containing the information we have on an SUV and its occupants — the people who grabbed Gordon

Strachan from outside of the Last Drop. Make sure you feature it in your articles and news items, get it circulated. We need these twisted criminals off our streets as soon as possible."

MᴄKᴇɴᴢɪᴇ's ꜰᴏʀᴇʜᴇᴀᴅ had broken out in sweat. He wiped it with his handkerchief, hands still shaking.

"I'm sorry, Grant..." DS Robertson placed a hand on his arm. "Can I get you something? A cup of tea, just until Graham gets back?"

He shook his head. "No, thank you, Susan." He checked his watch. "I think we should head up there."

Graham was back; panting from running up the full flight of stairs. "They were right... they found a body atop Arthur's Seat. Would you like me to drive?" The DC's face lined with concern. "Och, I'm really sorry, sir..."

McKenzie thought of his sister and her family. How was he going to tell her? He ran a hand through his hair, his breathing ragged. "Aye, Graham, you can drive. I couldn't trust myself to right now."

He didn't notice the roads, the people, or the buildings they passed. All was a vague blur beyond his thoughts; beyond the dread he felt.

When they arrived at St Margaret's Loch, McKenzie took off his seatbelt; opening the car door before Dalgleish had turned off the engine.

The three officers ran up the path to Arthur's Seat, the DI leading the way. Ahead, he recognised the familiar shape of his sister and her husband. "Och, no," he said aloud. "Davina!" He slowed as he neared her.

She turned to look at him, tears streaming down her face.

He placed a hand on each of her shoulders. "Is it him?"

She let out a howl. "I don't know. They're all saying it's him."

"I'm so sorry, sis, but you cannot go up there. It's likely a crime scene, and we have to keep it sterile."

"We have to know if it's him," her husband Jim objected.

"I will go." Grant's voice was firm. "I will come right back here and let you know, I promise."

Davina appeared torn and, for a moment, McKenzie thought she was going to continue on up the hill. But she stayed, sobbing into her husband's shoulder.

"Please hurry." Jim locked eyes with the DI. "Let us know if it is our boy."

The detectives continued up to where a forensic team had pegged out the approach path, paramedics having confirmed the victim was lifeless.

As McKenzie drew near, he saw a full head of dark hair. His breath caught in his throat. "It's not him," he cried out, unable to hide his relief. "It isn't Goose." He approached the cordon, where he could see the face more clearly. "It's definitely not Gordon."

"You stay," Susan suggested. "I'll go let your sister know, and she can go home. She and her husband had a hell of a fright."

"Thank you, Sue," McKenzie answered, without turning round. His focus was on the dead man.

Graham joined him at the cordon, handing out plastic suits so they could view the body close up.

"I think he's wearing Goose's clothing..." The DI frowned, recognising the black paint splashes on the side of one of his nephew's Nikes. That, and the blue-check lumberjack shirt, were almost certainly Gordon's. "Why is he wearing my nephew's clothes?" He rubbed his forehead. "Where is Goose?"

The victim's shirt was blood-soaked, as were the top and thighs of his blue jeans. And blood had splashed onto the tops of the trainers.

Paramedics, carrying their kit, set off for the path back down from the rock.

McKenzie strode towards them, his plastic suit crackling. He pulled down his face mask. "Was he shot?"

The nearest medic shook his head. "It looks like multiple stab wounds, but the pathologist will have the final say. There's so much blood, and wounds can be deceptive. But I believe the killers used a bladed weapon. Judging by the blood on the ground, they killed him where he fell."

"Yes, I saw that. Thank you." The DI turned his face towards the city, stretching into the distance below the mound. He noticed the chill wind for the first time. It was a cold and lonely place to die. McKenzie could only imagine the horror of the victim's last moments. He didn't want to think about it, but it was his job to do so. And it was their task to tackle the horror while everyone else walked away. He brought his eyes back to the dead man.

"Poor Bastard, eh?" Dalgleish shook his head.

"Let's hope we get his identity soon. We need a time of death from the pathologist. The killers will be long gone back to their holes. But how is my nephew connected to the victim? I bet whoever murdered this lad knows where Goose is."

"I'll make sure we have CCTV from the approaching streets, and any dash cam footage from passing cars."

"Aye, we can't achieve much more up here. Let's get back and get this murder investigation underway. We must find this killer or killers before they do it again. Before they do the same to..." He didn't need to say anymore. They both knew who he was referring to.

6

AN ANXIOUS TIME

D I Grant McKenzie sat in the cosy living room of his Victorian home in The Grange, surrounded by the tranquillity typical of this leafy residential area in Edinburgh. It was a far cry from the rougher parts of the city. Soft evening sunlight filtered through the curtains, casting an orange glow on the space. His wife, Jane, sleeves rolled up and dark hair in a ponytail, took a break from the kitchen and joined him on the couch. Concern furrowed her forehead as they discussed the guilt Grant felt over spending time with her and the children, when his sister was so distressed and his nephew was still out there somewhere.

The DI leaned back, fingers unconsciously drumming on the armrest of the chair. "I really don't know what to make of it. Gordon's disappearance and the poor lad found up on Arthur's Seat in Goose's clothing... It's a crazy twist I wasn't expecting... I thought the worst when they said a body had been found on Arthur's Seat, and the clothing matched Gordon's. I braced myself for the worst."

Jane inclined her head, her gaze a mix of sympathy and

support. She reached out a hand, placing it on his knee. "I can't even imagine what your sister and nephew are going through. But you know, people can do surprising things... Stuff that is out of character. Do you think there could be a connection between Gordon and the victim's murder? I mean, because of the clothes..."

Grant's gaze dropped to the floor, his mind racing. "I want to believe Gordon is innocent, and that he wouldn't be involved in something like this. But you're right, people hide things from each other all the time. What if he was there? It's just... It really isn't like him to get mixed up with the wrong crowd. Besides, we have CCTV footage of him being taken. If he faked it, I would know. Wouldn't I?"

Jane's voice was gentle. She could see how torn her husband was. "You can't carry the weight of this on your shoulders. You're a brilliant detective, but you're also a father. Craig, Martha, and Davie need you, too. And you are close to this case... Too close, perhaps."

He sighed. "I know, love. I think Sinclair will take me off the case the minute he realises the victim was wearing Gordon's clothing."

"Would that be so bad?"

He ran both hands through his hair. "I promised Davina. But, yes, I know how preoccupied I've been with this case and I've barely had time with the children. They've been asleep by the time I've come home every night this week. I'm surprised they still recognise me."

Jane squeezed his knee. "Then, for tonight, let's focus on being here with them. We'll enjoy these moments, and you can tackle Gordon's disappearance again tomorrow. I know you're worried, but if you let it consume every minute of your time with our children, you will regret it."

He managed a smile, grateful for his wife's insight. She

had a knack for cutting through the chaff; clarifying his thoughts. "You're right. I need to be here for Craig, Martha, and Davie. They're growing up so fast."

As if on cue, the sound of laughter and footsteps approached the living room door. Moments later, the three children burst into the room. Their faces lighting up on seeing their parents together; their enthusiastic playfulness, infectious.

"Dad! Mam! Look what we made in school today!" Davie exclaimed, waving a cardboard aeroplane in his hand.

Grant held it up, zooming it through the air; making deep engine sounds. "Wow, I've never seen such a fine model. It must have taken you all day, eh?" He grinned, winking at Jane.

Martha showed them a colourful drawing she had done, and Craig chimed in with tales of a soccer match he had played with his friends. During those precious hours, the investigation took a backseat as Grant immersed himself in the joy and innocence of family. Tomorrow would be different, but tomorrow could wait.

THE DI STEPPED into the sterile, white-tiled environment of the mortuary at Western General Hospital. The air felt cold and clinical, a stark contrast to the warmth of the home he had left only an hour ago. He was there to see the autopsy of the victim found on Arthur's Seat, hoping the pathologist's insights would provide some clarity to the puzzling case consuming his thoughts.

Fifty-year-old Dr Fiona Campbell, the hospital's experienced pathologist, stood at a stainless steel table, already prepped in a surgical gown, gloves, and face shield. The victim, a twenty-four-year-old male, lay on the cold steel table, shrouded in a white sheet.

Grant's stomach clenched on seeing the lifeless form, a stark reminder of the brutality which had occurred on Edinburgh's famous landmark.

"DI McKenzie," she acknowledged with a nod, her voice warm despite the sombre setting. "I'll be conducting the autopsy today. I hope we can shed light on the circumstances of his death. He was young."

Grant nodded, his eyes focussed on the table. "Twenty-four... It's no age to die."

As Dr Campbell began her investigation, the room hummed with the sound of equipment; the DI noting the subtle but familiar scent of disinfectant. He stood a respectful distance away, watching as the pathologist meticulously documented the victim's wounds, each incision and observation a step towards understanding what had transpired atop the old volcano.

"There are twelve penetrative wounds," she said, pushing the glasses up her nose with the back of a gloved hand. "Whoever did this clearly didn't want a quick death."

"What about the weapon?"

"Fixed blade, large, ten to twelve inches long, and with a serrated edge. Not the thing you want to come across out there."

"No..."

She worked with precision, carefully peeling back layers of skin and muscle to reveal the evidence hidden beneath. Grant's stomach churned, a mix of occupational curiosity and unease, as he watched her work. "Was it one weapon? Or multiple?"

"I think it may be the same weapon, but we'll have to run more tests. We'll get Luke, the forensic biologist, onto it." She continued. "Most of the stab wounds are to the chest and abdomen, consistent with the same sharp-bladed weapon. The assailant was quite determined. The wounds are deep; there's bruising from the impact of the hilt."

Grant swallowed. The brutality of the attack was evident. He cleared his throat, his voice steady despite the turmoil in his gut. "Do you know how long the assault lasted? There's no CCTV up there. You suggested it may have continued for a while?"

Dr Campbell paused, lifting her eyes to his. "It's hard to say definitively, but based on the wounds and extent of the bleeding, I'd estimate several minutes, at least. He bled out. The cause of death was cardiac arrest due to blood loss."

McKenzie considered this description of the victim's demise, witnessing the attack in his mind. He forced the unbidden image of his nephew, knife in hand, out of his head. That idea was ridiculous.

The pathologist meticulously collected samples, docu-mented injuries, and gathered evidence, providing a clear picture of the victim's last moments. The DI was glad he was merely an observer. It took a special person to do Dr Camp-bell's work, day-in; day-out. He admired Fiona, but he wouldn't want to wear her shoes.

After what felt like an eternity, she finally straightened, removing her gloves and face shield. She turned to him, removing her gloves. "We'll need to further analyse the samples and review the evidence with colleagues, but someone attacked this young man, inflicting multiple stab wounds. Bruising to his upper arms suggests at least two people held him while the attack took place. I believe you are looking for multiple offenders, Grant. This was likely the work of a gang."

"Thank you, Dr Campbell." He nodded, quietly anxious about Gordon. He couldn't let his nephew end up like this.

As he left the hospital mortuary, the autopsy's revelations weighed on him. The brutal nature of the victim's wounds was a stark reminder that his nephew was likely being held by dangerous and ruthless murderers. The sooner they located him, the better.

7

DEAD MAN'S BEEF

A biting wind cut through the air outside Leith Police Station, sending shivers down Grant McKenzie's spine as he walked up the steps to meet with the team. The warmth of the office, along with the focussed efficiency with which his team was working, helped lift his spirits.

Susan Robertson, Graham Dalgleish, and Helen McAllister waited in a corner of the briefing room to discuss the latest developments with him. He checked his watch. He was fifteen minutes late.

"Morning, everyone." He arranged his notes and box file on the table. "Thanks for coming. Let's get straight on with it."

Susan read from her notebook. "We received an update from Luke at the lab. They've identified the male victim found on Arthur's Seat as twenty-four-year-old Mark Anderson, identified via his fingerprints. He had a history of petty offending since his teens, mainly shoplifting and minor drug possession. Though I see nothing in his past that would single him out as a candidate for murder. No history of gang-affiliation or the like."

Grant smoothed his beard. "We should go through known associates. Find out which of them had contact with him in the last days and weeks of his life."

Graham chimed in. "Sounds like he might have gotten in with the wrong crowd. Perhaps he was running drugs for a gang."

Helen McAllister looked up from her notes. "The DCI says he wants us on top of this. He's under pressure from community leaders. He says we're being closely watched."

Grant nodded agreement. "Sinclair's right, we're in the spotlight with this one. Arthur's Seat is popular with locals and tourists alike. The last thing we need is more victims, and my nephew is still missing."

"No news?" Dalgleish cocked his head. "Jeez, I'm sorry, Grant. Your family must be beside themselves."

"My sister isn't sleeping, as you might expect. But, if we find out who did this to Mark Anderson, it could lead us to whoever is holding Gordon. Keep an eye out for anyone who had a grudge against Anderson, or anyone using the lad for their own ends," Grant suggested. "Even though his previous offences were minor, they could have brought him into contact with dangerous criminals."

Susan nodded. "Agreed. There's CCTV at the high rise where he was living. We've got officers going through it to see who was coming and going in recent days. According to the neighbours, there was bumping and banging at all hours, and people going back and forth from his flat."

"Good, let me know how that develops, and if you find anything interesting. I'm off to Sinclair's office. He wants to see me, apparently."

Graham pursed his lips. "Aye, sir. Good luck with that."

"Let's get to work," Grant said, his tone resolute. "We owe it to Mark and his family to uncover the truth behind his death."

McKenzie lingered after the others left. Although the warmth of the station had vanquished the chill in his back, he had a feeling the atmosphere would be less than cosy in the DCI's office.

Jock Munro sat alone in the bar of the Last Drop tavern, ahead of the lunchtime rush. He was one of only a handful of patrons; the others talking at tables.

The Twenty-year-old wanted to be alone; to stare into his beer, remembering the night Gordon was abducted. He jiggled his knee up and down repeatedly, sighing now and then.

Shania McInnes was once more behind the bar; flicking through a local newspaper while waiting to serve the next customer. When she finished, she began folding it.

"Wait, can I see that?" Jock held out his hand.

"Sure..." She shrugged, passing it over. "Fill your boots."

It was the photograph on the front that caught his attention. A young man smiling from the page, the one found murdered on Arthur's Seat. Jock's forehead furrowed, sure he recognised the face. He tried to remember where he had seen it. When realisation dawned, he fished out his mobile to call McKenzie.

THE DI'S PHONE RANG, interrupting the steady hum of activity in the main MIT office at the Leith Police station. He picked up the call. "Grant McKenzie."

"Mr McKenzie, it's Jock," came the voice on the other end. "Gordon's best friend..." The urgency in the young man's tone was palpable, even through the phone line.

The DI leaned forward in his chair. "What's going on? Has he turned up?"

"No... I'm sorry, he hasn't. But I'm at the Last Drop," he explained, a tremor in his voice. "I saw something in the paper."

"Go on..."

The lad's words came in a nervous rush. "I saw a photograph of the guy they found dead on Arthur's Seat. I know him, sir. Or at least, I knew I'd seen him before. He's the one who bumped into Gordon a few days before Goose went missing. The one who almost knocked him over, and they exchanged words."

Grant frowned as he connected the dots. He remembered Jock mentioning the encounter the last time they spoke. "Are you sure it's the same man?"

"Yeah, I'm positive," Munro replied. His voice calmed following the revelation. "I recognised him from the photograph in the Daily Record. It shook Gordon up... He wasn't himself after their argument in the street. After the spat, the Anderson lad walked off. I didn't think too much of it then, but now... Well, what with him being found in Gordon's clothes... I think there must be a connection with his disappearance."

The DI checked his watch. "Stay where you are. I am coming to see you. I'll be right there."

Tense, McKenzie grabbed his coat and headed for the door. The memory of his nephew's face and the photograph of the murdered man mingled in his mind. The Last Drop was a short drive away, but it felt longer. He was desperate to know more about the street encounter between Goose and the dead man.

The pub was busy now, its patrons engrossed in conversation and laughter. Grant spotted Jock sitting at the bar, and walked over, sliding into the seat next to Goose's friend, his voice low as he spoke. "Tell me everything, Jock. Every detail about that encounter between Gordon and Mark Anderson."

Munro recounted what he remembered about the incident, his words punctuated by frustration and regret. Grant listened intently, taking it all in. On its face, the encounter was a spur-of-the-moment thing. An argument over a clumsy clash of shoulders. But could there have been more to it?

Munro shrugged. "It might be nothing, but something within me says it's too much of a coincidence." He downed the rest of his pint.

Grant's eyes locked with the lad's. "No detail is too small, Jock. I'm glad you called me. It could be something or nothing, I agree. But it is likely significant, especially since Anderson was wearing Goose's clothes when they found him. But I can tell you this much... the whole situation is confusing as hell."

MCKENZIE LEANED back in his chair, one of the few officers remaining, as late afternoon became early evening. His tortured mind grappled with the investigation, the stack of papers on his desk a stark reminder of the growing task they faced. His gaze wandered over photographs on the white-

board. The ones capturing the grimness of the scene atop
Arthur's Seat; the bloody mess that was the Mark Anderson's body and the sodden earth around it.

The DCI was waiting. He'd been putting the meeting off,
afraid of what his superior might say. Grant checked his
watch. It was now or never.

He rapped his knuckles lightly on the open door of the
SIO. Sinclair was a seasoned officer, known for his method-
ical approach to cases, but there was something different
about his demeanour today, and the DI could take a good
guess at why. The lack of greeting from Sinclair increased
the tension in McKenzie's shoulders.

He pushed his hands deep into his trouser pockets and
swallowed hard. "Rob... You wanted to see me?"

Sinclair sighed, his gaze on the photographs lying across
his desk. His way, perhaps, of preparing the DI for what he
was about to say. "I've reviewed the evidence. The murder
victim wore clothing belonging to your nephew. And
Gordon, as we know, is AWOL."

McKenzie cleared his throat. "Look, I understand how
this would make you concerned about my involvement with
the case. But I know Gordon and have insights others don't."
He grimaced, his brain searching for the words to convince
the DCI. "I know the clothing complicates things, sir, but I'm
as committed as anyone to finding the truth. I won't let
personal ties cloud my judgment... You know I won't."

Sinclair's gaze met McKenzie's, his red nose crinkling as
he studied him. "I'm not questioning your dedication, but
the circumstances make it complicated. Your connection
could damage your judgement and the objectivity you need,
regardless of whether you think they will."

Leaning on his superior's desk, McKenzie wasn't about
to give up. "Look, I've formed relationships with witnesses,

sir. They're opening up; sharing details that might otherwise slip through the cracks. They trust me, and that trust will be essential if we are going to solve this. The murder was likely the work of a serious criminal gang. People are scared, most especially the youngsters. And we need them talking."

Sinclair pursed his lips, a sign of lingering skepticism. "I get that... But imagine if things take an even darker turn. Questions about your impartiality will be unavoidable. And what if the worst happens to your nephew? I know you don't want to contemplate that, but it is a distinct possibility. Would you want to spend the rest of your life wondering if your involvement in the case was a factor in Gordon's death?"

McKenzie's fingers tightened around the edge of the desk. "I won't let that happen. Not on my watch."

Sinclair reclined in his chair, arms folded. "You may not have a choice. As it stands, his fate is not in your hands. And what if he turns out to be the killer?" He reached for a tumbler and poured a measured amount of amber liquid, the scent of Dalmore single malt filling the room.

The DI glanced at the clock. It was seven o'clock already. Jane would be wondering where he was. "All I ask is that you think about it. I can take a back seat... I'll stay away from the cameras. You can deal with the press. I only want to talk to the kids out there. I'm sure they know something."

"I tell you what..." Sinclair knocked back the rest of his drink. "I'll let you continue, for now, while I think about it. But remember, I'll be watching you closely. The instant I sense you losing rationality, I won't hesitate to reevaluate your role."

McKenzie nodded, a mix of gratitude and relief on his face. "Thank you... You won't regret it. I'll treat this case as I would any other."

As he exited Sinclair's office, the DI knew he was treading a delicate line. The thinnest ever. A murderous gang, a missing nephew, and the expectations of family and the community were a formidable challenge. But it was one he was determined to meet head-on.

8

A WORLD OF MURK

McKenzie pushed open the door of the Elite-Fusion gym on his way to see another friend of Gordon's, Michael Murray, who worked there as a personal trainer.

The gym sat in the picturesque and historical location of West Richmond Street, which sported a mix of commercial and residential properties. The entrance was in a backstreet, through a close, near to both the University of Edinburgh and the Royal Mile.

The musky odour from those working out mingled with the smell of fresh laundry from the towels piled on one side of the counter.

"Can I help you?" the buff young man behind the desk enquired.

McKenzie flashed his badge. "DI McKenzie, I'm here to speak with Michael Murray. He said he would be here?"

"Oh, aye..." The lad pointed to the door ahead. "Through there... He'll be the one in the black vest top and shorts; dark hair."

"Got it, thank you." The DI pushed the door open,

scouring the patrons for the man fitting the description. He spotted him on a bench press near the back and strode over.

He showed his ID, and Murray sat up, mopping his face, neck, and biceps with a towel. "Mike?"

"Aye, that's me. So, you'll be McKenzie, eh?"

"DI McKenzie, yes. I'm here to talk about Gordon."

"Aye, I know. Have you found him yet?"

The DI shook his head. "No... I understand you are a friend of his?"

"I am. We go back a way. I'm still in shock that he's disappeared like this."

"Have you heard from him?"

"Not since he went from outside of the Last Drop. Jock said someone took him. Snatched him, he said."

"That's right, and it is vital we find out who these people are as soon as we can."

"Aye, of course."

"I understand you were there that night... at the Last Drop?"

"I was."

"Were you talking to Gordon?"

"Aye, I spoke with him for a bit. He was chatting with Jock mostly, but we did banter for a few minutes at one point."

"How was he?"

Murray ran a hand through obsidian-black hair. "He was all right. There was nothing up with him at all. I think he was building up the confidence to talk to a lassie he likes. The one who sometimes works behind the bar."

"Shania?"

"Yeah, that's her. She's a bit out of his league, eh? But he was gonna try with her, anyway. Braver man than me..."

"Why do you say that?"

"Well, you know, she's the sort of girl you can look at but not touch, if you get my drift. A bit on the chilly side, I would say. She gives you one of those looks that freezes your blood. I've seen it for myself. And I don't usually find it hard to pick up a girl, if you get what I mean." He felt his own biceps. "Not with these guns." He gave McKenzie a wink.

The DI stifled a grimace. "I thought you worked here?"

"Aye, I do. I am on a break, so I thought I'd put in some reps. It's gone quiet. Maybe they heard you coming, eh?"

"Did Goose tell you he liked Shania?"

"He talked about her a lot. I think he told Jock. The rumour is..." Murray checked himself.

"The rumour is what?"

"Well, I dunnae know if I should say..."

"You've started, so you might as well finish."

"Well, they say he liked a lass on the internet. A girl who does videos and stuff."

"What sort of videos?"

"Web chats."

"You mean chatting to men for money?"

"Aye, I think Goose was a customer. I got the impression the girl earned good money that way. Not that I would know..."

"Are we talking about Shania?"

Murray shrugged. "I don't know. Goose was too much of a gentleman to name and shame a girl."

"You said, was..." McKenzie frowned.

"Did I? Must have been a slip of the tongue. I meant is... He *is* too much of a gentleman to watch and tell."

"Do you know where Gordon is? Or what has happened to him?"

"You already asked me that, and I told you I don't. I was sitting at a table with everyone else when he disappeared. I wasn't looking through the window or anything. And I couldn't hear anything above the noise in the pub."

"Would you tell me if you knew something?"

"Aye, of course I would."

"What sort of web chats are they?"

"The girls banter, role play, and interact one-on-one with the guys on the web."

"Are they working for someone?"

"I think so."

"Who?"

Murray turned his eyes away. "I wouldn't know."

"You seem to know a lot, but not who the girls are working for?"

"No."

McKenzie cocked his head. "What if it had something to do with Gordon's disappearance? Would that jog your memory?"

"If you don't know, you don't know." Murray brought his stoney gaze back to the DI.

McKenzie cleared his throat. "Have a think about it, and if you hear a name connected with the girls, you let me know... Unless you think they work independently?"

He shrugged.

"What about the girl? Would Jock know her identity?"

"I dunnae ken. You'd have to ask him. He is closer to Gordon than anyone."

"I will."

"If you see Goose's mam? Give her my best. Tell her I hope he comes home soon."

The DI narrowed his eyes, unsure if Murray was genuine. "Aye, I will." He was about to leave, but turned back. "Do they charge a lot? The girls?"

He grinned. "Why, you thinking of trying them out later? I think your wife would have something to say about that."

"Very funny... I'd like an answer."

"I've heard of lads getting into debt... And I've heard of grown men handing over their life savings, and going broke. They fall in love, you see? Some guys think the girl feels the same way they do. It's easy for the man to forget she might talk to dozens or even hundreds of guys in a week. If you indulge in that sort of thing, do it with your eyes open."

"I'll see myself out." McKenzie turned on his heel. "You had better get off of that bench press. You've got clients waiting."

McKenzie checked his watch. He ought to be back at the station within the hour, but he wanted to stop by the Last Drop. He did not know whether Shania was working this morning, but would go there on the off-chance.

Lucky for him, she was behind the bar; hair held back in a French plait, talking with a male member of staff.

As the DI approached, she rocked forward on her stool, sitting upright. Her eyes narrowed as though preparing to shield herself from questions.

He held up his badge. "DI McKenzie, I-"

"I know who you are. I thought I told you what I know? And it's not much. I have no idea where Gordon Strachan is."

"I wanted to ask you about Mark Anderson."

"Anderson?" She frowned.

"Aye, we found him deceased on Arthur's Seat... Murdered."

She swallowed hard, her eyes flicking sideways,

checking whether her male colleague had overheard. But he was away wiping tables and appeared oblivious.

"You know anything about that?"

"No... Why would I?"

"Did you know Mark Anderson?"

"I might have done."

"Meaning?"

"I might have seen him in here. I've served many people in this pub."

"Had you heard about the body on Arthur's Seat?"

"Aye, I saw it on the news this morning. I thought it was sad." She lowered her gaze.

"And did you recognise him? They showed his picture."

She shrugged. "I felt like I had seen him somewhere before." She chewed her bottom lip. "How did he die? They didn't say on the news."

"We're keeping injury details under wraps, for now. We don't want to compromise our investigation."

"I see..."

"Was he here the night Goose was abducted?"

"Who, Anderson?"

"Aye."

"I can't remember. What was he wearing when you found him? If you describe his clothing..."

McKenzie studied her face as he answered. "He wore Gordon's lumberjack shirt, jeans, and trainers."

Her eyes widened; mouth falling open. She snapped it shut. "Oh."

"That's odd, don't you think? What would Anderson be doing wearing Gordon's clothes, unless they had both been in contact with Anderson's killer?"

"Unless..." She frowned. "Unless..."

"Go on..."

"Gordon killed Anderson?"

The DI held her gaze. "Why would Gordon do such a thing?"

"I don't know." She swallowed. "It was just a suggestion, is all."

McKenzie mulled over what Jock had said regarding the altercation between Goose and Anderson in the street, days before the latter's death. "Did they have a beef with each other?"

Shanie shrugged. "How would I know?" She regarded him through lowered lashes.

McKenzie thought he caught a tremor in her upper lip. "You would tell me if you were aware of trouble between the two of them, wouldn't you?"

"Of course." She swallowed again.

"Gordon was apparently following a girl online." The DI inclined his head.

"Really? I wonder who that was?" she asked, grabbing a beer cloth from on top of the bar and wiping the already clean; dry surface. "I wouldn't know anything about that either."

"Were you aware he also liked you?"

"Me?" She frowned.

"Aye, he was looking for a way to ask you out."

She wrinkled her nose. "I would have turned him down. We don't..." She closed her mouth again.

"You don't what?" He asked. "Cavort with clients?"

"What are you insinuating? What do you take me for?"

Her vehemence took him by surprise. He didn't wish to push things too early. Perhaps she should stew for a while. He held up his hands, palm outwards. "Hey, hey... take it easy... It's my job to ask questions. You tell me what you were about to say when you stopped yourself, and I won't make assumptions."

"I can't remember. I lost my thread." She looked at him as though he was stuck to the bottom of her shoe. "I'm sorry, was there anything else? I've got work to do."

He watched her hand continue polishing an already shiny bar. "Aye, I can see that."

"We'll be getting busier any minute now."

He checked his watch. It was eleven already. Lunchtime punters would start pouring in soon. "Aye, all right. I'll leave you to it. But if you remember any more about Gordon or Mark Anderson, please call me. Here's my number..." He handed her a card. "We don't want Gordon ending up in the same condition we found Anderson, do we? Think about it."

"SHE'S HIDING SOMETHING," McKenzie said to Dalgleish, as the latter handed him a steaming brew.

"Who is?"

"Shania McInnes... She knows more than she's saying. Go through her social media... TikTok, Instagram; anything else she is using. Find out who she talks to, and why."

"You sound like you are onto something. Have you got a lead?"

He shrugged. "Maybe... Mike Murray, one of Gordon's friends, claims Goose was paying for web chats with a young woman."

"Oh..." Dalgleish pursed his lips. "You mean like 'Only Fans'?"

"Something like that, yes."

"Have you asked your sister?"

"Davina? Not yet. I've been debating how to broach the

subject with her. I have a feeling the discussion might not go down too well."

"Aye, she might not take too kindly. Especially when he's missing. She probably thinks butter wouldn't melt-"

"My sister isn't naïve, Graham."

"No, I didn't mean to imply..."

"Sorry..." McKenzie sighed. "I'm a wee bit fraught, as you can probably see. I am scared for my nephew's safety, and apprehensive of what I might find down this rabbit hole."

"What do you mean?" Dalgleish frowned.

"I hope he's not had anything to do with Mark Anderson's death."

"Because Anderson was wearing his clothes?"

"Aye, and don't tell me that thought hasn't crossed your mind, too."

Dalgliesh looked at his shoes. "It is difficult to explain."

"There you go... See? I knew it... But I can't blame you. I am just as concerned about that, and the fact they had a head-on collision in the street and exchanged words. This doesn't look good for Gordon."

"They were in a car crash?" Dalgleish scratched his head, eyebrows raised.

"No, they bumped into each other walking along the Royal Mile. They were on a night out with friends. It happened around closing time."

"Ah, I see."

The DI rubbed his chin. "I'm so tired, I canna see the wood for the trees. But I'll go see my sister tonight... See if she can shed any light on who this web-chat lassie is. But, if this girl was charging Goose and others money for time or anything else, I'll bet ten-to-one she won't be in it alone. There will be some overlord... Some kingpin pocketing the lion's share of the revenue."

Dalgleish nodded. "Aye, that's usually the way it works. It's a murky world, Grant; dangerous, too. You should go canny if Goose has got himself involved in something like that."

McKenzie sighed. "I am afraid... Not for myself, but for Gordon and my sister."

"I'll see what I can find out about Shania McInnes this afternoon. We can catch up later, after you've talked with Davina."

McKenzie gave Dalgliesh a nod. "Thanks, Graham. Speak later."

9

STOLEN MONEY

McKenzie pushed open the creaky gate leading to his sister's house in Morningside. Even before he rang the doorbell, he sensed a tension in the air. Someone had left the door an inch ajar. He pushed it open and wandered in, finding Davina seated near the living room window, her eyes red from crying; a used Kleenex crumpled in her right hand.

"Sis?" his voice was soft as he took a seat across from her. "How are you holding up?" He cleared his throat, placing a warm hand on hers, for once unsure of his words.

She offered him a shaky smile and blew her nose into the tissue. "As well as is possible, I suppose."

He leaned forward, concern lining his forehead. "I need to ask you more questions about Gordon. I know this is a difficult time, but we are exploring several leads."

Davina nodded, her sore eyes lifting to his. "Of course... Anything to help bring Goose back. Is there news? What new leads?"

McKenzie cleared his throat. "Did you notice whether

he was spending unusual amounts of money before he disappeared? Did he ask you for any?"

Davina swallowed, turning her gaze towards the window.

Grant waited, sensing her reluctance and the instinct to protect her son.

"He was spending money, yes." She ran her hands through mussed hair. "I didn't want to say anything at first. I mean, he helped his dad out when things needed doing in the house or garden and Jim gave him money. Gordon topped that up by helping in bars, pulling pints when they were short-staffed. He seemed to have more money than usual, but he also seemed to go through that money in next to no time. I had hoped he would save extra cash for when he was at university. He'll need it while he's on his course."

Grant raised a brow. "Do you have any idea where the extra money came from?"

Davina hesitated before answering, her voice barely above a whisper. "I assumed it was from the bars he helped. He didn't tell me much." Her face contorted.

"Sis? What is it?" The DI leaned in. "What's the matter?"

"He used my credit card... Twice, that I know of. He spent hundreds of pounds each time. I don't know what he bought. He wouldn't tell me. I thought he might be gambling, but he denied it every time I asked."

Grant's forehead furrowed. "He used your credit card without your permission?"

Davina nodded, tears glistening in her eyes. "Yes...We had a huge row about it. I was so angry. Jim was even more cross than I was. He called Goose ungrateful and threatened to report him to the police. But... now I just want him back, Grant. I don't care about the money. I love my son and want him home." Silent tears rolled down her cheeks. "Please bring him back to us."

He placed an arm around her shoulder. "We'll do everything we can to get him back."

"What has he got himself mixed up in?" she asked, pain hollowing her eyes. She took a shaky breath. "Do you think he was being blackmailed? I still don't understand why he stole from us like that."

McKenzie chose his next words carefully. "It's a possibility we will explore, Davina. Knowing what he was involved in prior to the abduction may increase our chances of locating him. We are exploring several scenarios. The more we know, the better."

She nodded. "Thank you... I appreciate all you are doing for us. I really do."

"I'm as desperate to find Goose as you are." He sighed. "But hold nothing back from me. I know you have agonised over telling me about the stolen money on your credit card, but those sorts of details could be pivotal to finding Gordon."

As the conversation dwindled into an uneasy silence, Grant's thoughts wandered to a darker possibility. He had a hunch, but wasn't ready to share it with his already distraught sister. "Believe that we're looking into every angle. But, if you remember anything else, no matter how small, please tell me. It all adds up, giving us a clearer picture of what we are dealing with."

She nodded, turning to the window, and the black clouds gathering outside. "I will... Just bring him home safe, please."

Her words hung heavy as McKenzie walked back to his car. Her desperate plea tugged at his core. As he fired up the engine of the Audi, he spoke his thoughts aloud. "Keep strong, Sis. Trust that we will find him."

HE ENTERED the dimly lit Last Drop tavern, the familiar aroma of stale beer and old wood wafting in the air. His eyes scanned the room until they landed on Shania McInnes behind the bar. She was wiping down glasses with a practiced mechanical efficiency.

Well-worn carpeting muffled his footsteps. "Shania?"

Her startled reaction surprised him. What was she so nervous about?

She stared at him wide-eyed, a mixture of surprise and apprehension crossing her features. "DI McKenzie? What do you want?"

"Well, that's no way to greet someone." He leaned against the bar, his gaze steady. "I wanted to talk to you. Have you time?"

The girl hesitated, her gaze eyes shifting around the room. She set the glass down under the bar. "What's it about?" She pushed stray hair behind her ear, shifting the weight between her feet.

"We've been hearing things, Shania... About your online activities."

She swallowed hard, looking around her. "Keep your voice down. I don't know what you're talking about. I don't do stuff like that."

"Like what?"

"Like what you said."

"I wasn't specific."

She pulled a face. "I enjoy working here. Please don't mess it up for me."

Grant's expression remained calm. "Look, we don't want to have a detrimental effect on your employment. But I need to talk to you."

"Fine," she said, leading him further along the bar to ensure they wouldn't be overheard. "What are you asking?"

"Are you chatting with men online for money?"

"No, I'm not. Why would I do anything like that? Why do you even think that?"

He held her gaze, his eyes searching for signs of deception. "One young man is missing, and another is now dead. I need you to be honest with me."

After a tense moment, she frowned. "It's not like you think. I need the money. God knows this job doesn't pay me nearly enough. You know, a lot of women do this sort of thing now. I'm not the only one. Not by a long shot."

"Do you pocket all the money yourself?" He cocked his head, his expression thoughtful, giving her time.

She chewed her lower lip.

"Are you doing this on your own, or are you working for someone else? A gang, maybe?"

Shania's gaze flickered with uncertainty, her eyes darting back and forth. "I can't tell you that... You don't understand. When you leave here, you go back to your police station fortress with your electronic key fobs and heavily armed officers. But what the hell protection do I have? You don't know these people. You don't know what they're capable of. I have family..."

"Then tell me."

She continued glancing around the tavern. "Listen, the danger is out there, and it's real. I talk to you, I get messed up. That's the way it is."

Grant leaned in, his voice gentle but firm. "Shania, you

don't have to be alone in this. If there's something going on, tell us. We can help you."

She stopped talking and stared at the counter.

"Is Gordon Strachan one of your customers?"

"Don't say it like that," she hissed.

"Then how should I say it?" He pulled back. "Shania, it's important. We cannot find Goose if we don't know what he had gotten himself into."

Shania's lips trembled. "Look, I do web cam work for money. But I can't say who I'm working for, and I can't tell you where the money goes. They pay me a commission for the videos, but most of it goes elsewhere."

"How much of it goes elsewhere?"

She shrugged. "Seventy percent? Something like that."

"How is the money paid?"

"We have a payment app."

"Is it paid to you first? Or the people you work for?"

"I don't work for them... I work with them. It's an agreement." Her voice trailed away, as though she was unsure of what she was saying.

Grant's brow furrowed. "Shania, you understand this could be dangerous. I can see that you do. If someone is exploiting you and others like you, we should put a stop to it."

Her gaze hardened, a mixture of defiance and worry in her eyes. "You think I don't know that? But I won't risk my family's safety. And I don't know if I can trust you to keep your word."

"You didn't tell me which way the money flows?"

"The patrons pay it to me. It shows on the screen when they pledge it. The gang sees every amount that comes in, and they invoice for that amount at the end of the night."

"Do you do this every day?"

She shook her head. "They tell us when to work, and how long for. Sometimes they have specific customers lined up, and other times, we can talk to our personal fans. If they have specific clients in mind, they tell us how they want us to dress. You know, a bit of role play. Some guys like that sort of stuff. Like us to look innocent. And some of them prefer a rougher look." She coloured.

McKenzie nodded. "What about the men?"

"What about them?"

"Are any of them extorted? Or is the payment to girls the only time they give money?"

She shifted the weight between her feet, and began polishing the bar, her movements stiff, almost manic.

He cleared his throat. "You know we will do everything we can to protect you and your family, if you talk to us?"

"I have to work now," she said, standing up and folding her arms, the bar cloth still in her hand.

"Shania, we can find this information ourselves. But you could give us a head-start."

"It's all encrypted. They use VPNs."

"We have specialist teams. They are used to dealing with this sort of thing."

"Let me think about it?" She unfolded her arms, placing her hands on her hips. "I think you should go."

As he walked from the bar, Grant couldn't shake the feeling they had stumbled on a massive operation. A kingpin running an organisation that exploited vulnerable girls and extorted young men. McKenzie was determined to unmask this criminal enterprise and take the kingpin down.

10

DARK DEALINGS

The grand mansion exuded opulence and excess, a testament to its owner's power and influence. He had embellished modern furnishings with extravagant bling in a display of ostentation that could only belong to someone with an insatiable appetite for more.

The flooring was a mosaic of dark marbled tiles, intricately patterned in varying shades of grey that seemed to shift and shimmer on walking through the room. The occasional gold filigree entwined with the patterns, a touch of decadence in the otherwise monochrome expanse.

The man in charge sat one end of a large granite table. His staff scurried about, executing any command at a moment's notice. They moved with urgency, knowing a misstep would invite wrath from the one holding his subordinates in orbit, loyal and fearful.

The room was an intricate mix of voyeurism and power. Monitors spanned the walls, displaying live feeds from young women, captured in intimate moments through the webcams they used to interact with eager clients. Their suggestive dances met the lustful gazes of customers who paid whatever they could afford, and sometimes that included a lifetime's savings or even ill-gotten gains. The Man, as his subordinates referred to him, revelled in the staggering sums of money ticking away at the bottom of the live feeds, the riches streaming into his world.

His fingers moved with a sinister elegance, caressing a collection of lethal weapons. He toyed with a variety of knives and handguns with unsettling familiarity while a symphony played in the background. He brandished the instruments of destruction with casual disregard. A wave of his hand could herald devastation or death, a reminder that his power extended far beyond the screens that displayed tantalising performances.

When angry, his voice would cut the air like one of his blades, laced with venom or impatience, as he issued orders to the workers. They did as they were told, trapped by their fear of him and the unyielding grip of a criminal world many of them believed they would never escape. Some didn't want to. Their eyes were on coveted positions further up the food chain.

He frowned at a screen in the corner whose image was blank; the money at zero. "Where's Carla?" he barked, checking his watch. "She should have started her stream by now. Find out where she is and why she isn't working."

"Yes, boss." A muscular, bald-headed male left the room to make the calls.

The Man turned back to the blank screen, tapping the table with the point of a knife and tutting. Missed streams meant lost revenue, and perhaps lost clients. The girls were unwise to cross him, even one as beguiling as Carla.

GRAHAM DALGLEISH APPROACHED McKenzie's desk, shirt sleeves rolled up to the elbows. "I have an update on Anderson's phone, guv."

"Go for it." McKenzie leaned back in his chair, eyes fixed on the DC.

Dalgleish pulled out a tablet and tapped on it. "Forensics retrieved data from the cloud files associated with Anderson's mobile. It's not looking good for us, I'm afraid."

The DI's brow furrowed. "What do you mean?"

"Seems like someone got into the cloud after Anderson's death," Dalgleish showed him his screen. "They found evidence of unauthorised access, and it seems someone wiped many of the files."

McKenzie's jaw tightened. "I was worried they might do this."

"Yeah," Dalgleish ran a hand through his hair. "It's a sophisticated job, guv. Whoever did it knows their way around tech. They targeted files related to Anderson's contacts, messages, and recent internet activity."

McKenzie pursed his lips. "So they cleared the phone and erased the digital traces of Anderson's connections."

"Correct." Dalgleish nodded. "The techs salvaged a few fragments, so there is still hope," he added. "They found encrypted files, heavily protected. It's going to take some time to crack them. Whoever did this must have the money to pay hackers. This job would not have come cheap."

McKenzie drummed his fingers on his desk. "This was a clean-up job; a deliberate attempt to obscure Anderson's connections and activities. Whoever did this wants to stop us from finding out who he was communicating with."

"Whoever it was, wanted to remain in the shadows," Dalgleish agreed.

McKenzie's eyes narrowed. "Which brings us to the question of who would have the means and motive to orchestrate such a sophisticated hack?"

"The National Crime Agency suspects the involvement

of organised crime." Dalgleish leaned in. "They think this was to protect something bigger. Whatever the hackers are hiding must bring in a ton of money."

The DI's face darkened. "If the NCA is involved, then this is bigger than any of us expected. We ought to keep a lid on this, Graham. We can't tell the press about the hack. Let whoever is behind this think we don't know about it. I don't want to tread on the NCA's toes, but Susan and I will talk to Anderson's parents and ex-partner. Maybe they'll have names for us? Let's hope Anderson let something slip."

Dalgleish nodded. "I'll talk to the cybercrime unit to see if they can trace the unauthorised access, but I doubt it will be easy."

"We have to try," McKenzie said firmly. "We need to find out who Anderson was in contact with, what he knew, and why someone would go to such lengths to erase his digital footprint. Keep me updated on progress. And let's coordinate closely with the NCA. This investigation took a sharp turn into dangerous territory. I don't want any of our team at risk."

11

RIVALS FOR LOVE?

Mark Anderson's parents lived in a two-storey terraced home in Corstophine, a middle-income residential area in Edinburgh, with local amenities, and proximity to green spaces like Corstorphine Hill.

McKenzie and DS Susan Robertson drove via the periphery of the city centre to avoid the worst of the traffic. As they passed Murrayfield Stadium, Grant realised it had been a while since he had watched a big game. He would have to remedy that, and take his son Craig, the only one interested in rugby beside himself.

Twenty-four-year-old Anderson had moved back in with his mum and dad after splitting with his childhood sweetheart two months prior to his murder.

The detectives knocked on the door of the Victorian property and waited, their breath forming vaporous clouds in the chill, clear air.

A middle-aged man in a cotton shirt and corduroys opened the door with pronounced bags under his eyes. His glasses were atop his head. "Come in," he said, before they introduced themselves. "I'm Michael... My wife, Shirley, is in the sitting room."

"Thank you." McKenzie stepped back, allowing DS Robertson in first, glad of the protection his overcoat provided against the penetrating cold.

The interior of the Anderson residence was warm and inviting, a stark contrast to the wintry outdoors. The sitting room contained an eclectic mix of traditional and contemporary furnishings collected over decades. Grant rubbed his hands before holding them up to a fire crackling in the hearth.

"DI McKenzie and DS Robertson, is it?" Michael asked, his voice hoarse as though he had been crying. "Please, have a seat." He gestured toward a pair of armchairs facing a small pine coffee table.

"Thank you, Mr Anderson," The DI and Susan took their seats. "We appreciate your time."

Shirley's red-rimmed eyes were as tired-looking as her husband's. She rose from her place on the sofa. "Can we offer you something to drink? Tea? Coffee?"

"Not for me, thank you," DS Robertson responded.

"I'm okay." McKenzie held up his hand. "As you know, we're here to discuss your son, Mark. And I wanted to say how very sorry we are for your loss. I have children of my own, and I can only imagine the pain you have suffered."

The mention of their son's name cast a shadow over the couple. Michael's weary expression deepened, and Shirley's gaze fell to the floor, as though she were seeing her son as a small child.

"We understand Mark moved back in with you recently?" McKenzie leaned forward in his chair. "Could you tell us a wee bit about his circumstances?"

Shirley glanced at her husband, and Michael rubbed his

forehead before speaking. "Yes, our son had been living with us again," he said, his voice heavy. "He... He broke up with his childhood sweetheart, Carol, a couple of months ago. Mark came back with nothing. Not that Carol wanted to keep everything, just that he didn't want reminders of the relationship. It was as though he wished to erase it from his memory entirely. We found this odd, because they were well-suited and so in love, until something changed about six months ago."

His wife nodded in agreement. "He spent a lot of time in his room. It was a struggle to get him to interact with us, and others..."

McKenzie leaned forward. "Do you know the reason for the breakup?"

"Mark had become more private," Michael sighed. "He wasn't sharing with us anymore, especially regarding his relationship. He seemed... distant, and would be up in his room on his laptop, or out in Edinburgh."

DS Robertson pulled out her notebook. "When he went out, did he tell you where he was going, or who he was with?"

Michael shook his head. "No, not really... He would often come in and go straight to his room. My wife would call him for meals, and he would take them upstairs. We thought that odd. He had never been like that as a child. Even as a teenager, he would always eat his meals with us; never on his own."

"That's right," Shirley added. "Since he returned home, he spent a lot of time upstairs, on his laptop or watching TV."

"May we see his room?" McKenzie asked.

"Of course," Michael said, rising from his seat. "It's upstairs, the last door on the left."

They made their way up, footsteps creaking on the carpeted staircase.

Mark's room was neat and orderly, but devoid of personal touches. The furniture, though functional, lacked any sign of individuality.

The detectives knew forensic services had already been through the room, taking electronic devices. They would have the results of their investigations soon. The room felt desolate.

DS Robertson picked up a notepad from the desk, her gaze falling on the scribbles in the back. "There's a bunch of names in here, Grant... They include Kenneth Doyle and Shaun McNeil," she said, holding it up.

The DI walked across the room to look over her shoulder. "And Shania," he added, noting the overwriting and thickly penned letters. "Curious these names are here with no explanation why."

DS Robertson turned a page of the notepad, revealing indents from heavy writing. "It's as if he was thinking about Shania a lot."

"Could be relevant," McKenzie mused. "Perhaps he was a fan, like Gordon?"

"We should ask his parents if he was running short of money."

"Or if he asked them for any?" The DI nodded.

As they continued examining the room, it was clear the cleanliness of Mark's space was more a reflection of his mother's care than his own doing. The room otherwise appeared as though occupied by a transient guest, like Mark had seen it only as a crash pad.

"Let's see what forensics recover from his laptop. If there was a webcam connection, they should find it." DS Robertson turned her gaze to the window. "Such a shame he broke with his childhood sweetheart. Those webcam businesses destroy relationships."

McKenzie nodded. "And Shania isn't talking. She's too afraid of whoever she is working for."

"We could set up surveillance?"

He nodded. "I think the NCA will want to do that," he said.

"You told us Anderson bumped into Gordon in the street a few days before your nephew disappeared? If they both had their sights on Shania, that could be the reason for the altercation."

"But that would suppose they knew of each other?"

"Sure, but not necessarily about the watching her on screen. News travels fast amongst youngsters, especially with social media. And friends talk. Maybe they both knew of each other's crush on her... It was likely a topic for gossip."

McKenzie checked his watch. "We should leave... I'd like to speak to Anderson's ex-partner before lunch."

Susan nodded, pushing her hands into the pockets of her mac. "Let's go."

GRANT AND SUSAN arrived at Carol Galbraith's residence in Wester Hailes to the southwest of Edinburgh city centre, a traditional working-class area with a history of industrial and council housing development. It contained a mix of older buildings and modern construction. Over the years, the area had faced significant socio-economic problems, and parts were clearly run down.

Miss Galbraith lived in one of the older tenement buildings, in a tidy, one-bedroom apartment.

DS Robertson rang the bell.

Carol opened the door, her eyes puffy and red-rimmed; smoothing her skirt and shoulder-length dark hair with her hands. Her face was devoid of make-up. She glanced left and right along the street before inviting them in.

The detectives exchanged glances.

"Thank you for agreeing to see us, Miss Galbraith," McKenzie said, his voice low. "We appreciate your time."

The young woman led them to a small sitting area. Her hands shook as she offered them seats on a well-worn, grey tub sofa. She took a deep breath. "I miss him, but Mark changed so much over the last six months of our relationship. He was like a different person."

DS Robertson nodded. "In what way was he altered?"

Tears welled in Carol's eyes. "He started having mood swings, and would go from being loving and kind one moment to being abusive the next. He would shout and slam doors, making me feel like I wasn't good enough. Then afterwards, he would apologise and ask me for forgiveness, saying he wouldn't do it ever again."

McKenzie took notes, his expression serious. "Did he ever explain these episodes?"

Carol shook her head. "He was always pre-occupied, lost in his thoughts. I tried being patient, thinking he was going through a tough time, but it got worse. Eventually, he cut ties with me altogether, and with everyone... aside from his parents. He said he needed space. I think he was only civil to his mum and dad because he needed a place to stay."

"Was he using substances?"

"Drugs? Not as far as I know. But he had become distant... hard to read. He might have been using without me knowing it."

"Did he give you any reason for wanting to cut ties with you?" DS Robertson asked.

Carol's voice quivered. "No, he didn't. At first, it affected my sense of self-worth. I felt useless. Then I realised he was pushing everyone away, not only me. He was in his own world, and always on his laptop or phone."

McKenzie exchanged a glance with Robertson, both detectives sensitive to the woman's raw emotion. "Look, we know this must be difficult for you," he said.

She wiped her eyes with her sleeve. "I feel like I've been hit by a train. First he leaves, and then I find out someone stabbed him to death on Arthur's Seat. It all happened so fast. Too fast. And I don't know why any of it happened."

"We understand this is a lot for you to process," DS Robertson said gently. "Did Mark ever mention anyone who might have been causing him stress or trouble? Or any conflict he was involved in? Was he angry at anyone?"

Carol closed her eyes while she thought about it. "He didn't tell me, if he was. Looking back, I wish I could have done or said things that helped him... Something to make him stay, but he wouldn't let me in. And I was so upset and frustrated at him. I mean, his behaviour drove me crazy. I felt like I was losing my mind. Your feelings go numb after a while, and I guess mine did... Until they found him on Arthur's Seat. Then, all the pain came rushing back."

McKenzie nodded, his expression thoughtful. "In order to know what happened to Mark, we're exploring all avenues, and that includes speaking to everyone who was close to him, and anyone who might have wished him harm."

Carol's eyes widened, a mix of emotions flickering across her face. "Are you... Do you suspect me?"

Susan Robertson rubbed her chin. "We are not ruling anyone in or out at this stage."

"I see..."

"But is there anyone else you feel we should talk to?"

Carol shook her head. "I can't think of anyone."

The room fell silent.

McKenzie and DS Robertson exchanged a brief look before the DI spoke. "Just to clarify, Miss Galbraith, our job is to gather information and eliminate all potential leads. We're not for jumping to conclusions."

A tear streamed down Carol's cheek. "I loved Mark... Honestly, I did. Despite everything, I still cared about him. You must believe me. There's a killer out there..."

DS Robertson nodded. "We understand. We will uncover the truth and put whoever did this behind bars where they belong."

As the interview concluded, McKenzie had empathy for Carol's pain, but wondered if she knew more than she was saying. One thing he was sure about, however, Mark Anderson was not a happy man for many months prior to his death. The DI was determined to find out why.

12

EXTORTION

The evening was alive with conversation and the clinking of glasses as the team gathered at the Last Drop to celebrate DS Susan Robertson's thirty-fifth birthday. The pub's cordial ambience and sense of place provided a relaxed backdrop for some much-needed respite from the complex, demanding work of MIT. But despite enjoying the festivities, they never quite let go of the watchfulness that dwells in the blood of all detectives. McKenzie suggested the venue, as he wanted to observe the comings, goings, and interactions between the clientele.

At thirty-nine, everyone knew of Grant's intense dedication to the job. He stood tall at the bar, a good head and shoulders above the other patrons, his dark hair tousled, and piercing blue eyes shifting as he observed his colleagues and the other punters. As one of the youngest detectives to achieve the rank of DI, he had a reputation to uphold and took that seriously. He ordered the next round of drinks.

"Need a hand?" Dalgleish came to his aid. At forty-two, he was the elder statesman of the group. His sense of humour and easy smile belied his years of experience, though the grey developing at his temples gave him a knowledgeable air. Known for his dry wit and calm demeanour, Dalgleish's loyalty to the team was unwavering. He could occasionally be caught glancing at his phone. The screensaver was a photo of his wife and two grown-up daughters.

They carried the drinks back to the women.

DC Helen McAllister, with shoulder-length ash-blonde hair and thin-framed glasses, sat at the corner of the table. Her intelligence and attention to detail made her an invaluable asset to the team. But tonight, she was looking for a break from the case. Despite professional competence, her personal life was a puzzle she hadn't yet solved. Having tried her luck with dating apps like Tinder, she had taken a break from meeting men. Finding a connection that lasted beyond a few dates had proven elusive.

As they chatted over drinks, the conversation inevitably veered toward their personal lives. Helen took a sip of her drink and leaned back. "You know, it's difficult finding something meaningful these days. Dating apps are roulette wheels."

Susan chuckled. "Tell me about it. Before I met Greg, I'd interrogated some of my dates more thoroughly than suspects. It's hard to let down your guard when you do the job we do. Who here hasn't felt tempted to do a background check on a potential date?"

Dalgleish nodded agreement. "You think you've got everything figured out, and life throws a curveball..."

McKenzie took a sip of his pint of draught. "You seem pretty happy with your lot, though, Graham. Aren't you?"

"Och aye, of course. But there's always something needs doing at the house whenever I am working all hours on a case. It's always the way. When work is quiet, the house and kids behave."

"I thought your kids were all grown and settled at college?"

"Aye, they are... But they still call home when they need something, or when they need to bend our ear with the latest crisis. You never stop being a parent, do you?" He grinned at McKenzie. "You've got all this to come. Do you think you worry about them now? Wait until they get to their teens and go off in that car for the first time. Or come home and tell you their life is over because their latest love finished with them. Aye, you're forever fighting fires."

Susan, the birthday girl, chimed in with a wry smile. "Speaking of relationships, I've had enough curveballs to last a lifetime. Dave and I have our moments, but I can't imagine life without him."

"It must be hard when you both work shifts." Helen sipped her white wine. "I mean, the rest of us think it's a difficult balance when only one of us is working odd hours. But when there are two of you? I admire you for balancing that."

"It's difficult..." Susan stared into her glass. "But I wouldn't change Greg. He's honestly my rock. We've had our fights, but he is a gentleman through and through."

As the night continued, the team's conversation ebbed and flowed between personal anecdotes and lighthearted banter. They were close, their camaraderie cemented by the many challenges they had faced together. Occasionally, they slipped back into the job, scanning the room and watching the clientele.

Shania McInnes was not at the tavern tonight, either as a bartender or a customer. McKenzie made a mental note.

Helen glanced around and leaned towards him. "You can't stop, can you?"

He laughed. "I've seen you looking, too. We can never switch off, even on a night out."

Dalgleish raised his glass in a toast. "To you beggars... the best team on the force."

They chinked glasses, glad of their ability to laugh together even in the darkest of times. As the evening wound down, they paid the bill and made their way out of the pub, McKenzie's thoughts turning to his nephew.

As the city's lights glittered, sirens blared in the distance, a reminder their work never truly stopped.

McKENZIE AND DALGLEISH stood in front of the student digs in Marchmont, a vibrant neighbourhood south of Edinburgh University's central campus. The morning sun cast a pale glow over the scene. The previous night's festivities were a distant memory as they faced a new and sombre reality.

Dean Mitchell, a twenty-year-old mathematics student, had taken his own life with a cocktail of painkillers and whiskey. The body was discovered by a cleaner, who had gone home to recover from the shock.

McKenzie's head throbbed from the previous night's birthday celebrations. He rubbed his temples with his thumbs, trying to ease the pain as he prepared for the task at hand.

Dalgleish led the way through the corridor to the dorm.

The door to the young man's room was ajar, forensics officers assessing the scene. Although a suicide at first glance, they would treat the death as foul-play until the pathologist had completed the autopsy, especially since the room was in disarray. Someone had pulled drawers open, and scattered papers and belongings. It was unclear whether Dean was responsible for the mess, or a third party.

They suited up before going into where the student's body still lay, fully clothed, on the bed, one arm trailing on the floor, where lay the empty Glenfiddich bottle.

"Looks like someone was searching for something," Dalgleish remarked, scouring the room.

"Or sending a message," McKenzie added, his voice hushed. He approached the crime scene manager. "Are you guys developing fingerprints?"

She nodded. "But don't get your hopes up... Students are in and out of each other's rooms like flies." She pointed to the open drawers, some of whose contents had spilled to the floor. "What I can tell you is there are no prints on those... Not a one. Likely, whoever opened them wore gloves or wiped the handles afterwards."

"Maybe our boy here was murdered?"

"Or someone was afraid the death would attract attention to something they didn't want people to know?" She shrugged. "Let's see what comes out of the autopsy, eh? We'll gather the evidence we can."

McKenzie nodded, looking at the body of Mitchell. "Poor bugger... The problem is, at that age, they've no life experience. Nothing which tells them that no problem is ever that bad."

"His parents will be devastated."

"Aye, that they will. I don't envy the person informing them."

A reticent female student drew their attention. Standing near the doorway, her eyes darted around the room.

McKenzie approached her, his voice low. "Excuse me, miss?"

"Katherine MacLean. People call me Kat." She brushed shoulder-length blonde hair from her face. "My room is down the hall."

"Well, Miss MacLean, you can't come in. I'm DI McKenzie, and this is DC Dalgleish. We're investigators. Did you know the young man?"

Her gaze flitted between them, hands clasped together. "Yeah, I knew him. We shared some classes. He was a friendly lad. He didn't deserve this."

McKenzie nodded. "When did you last see him?"

"Yesterday. He left our lecture early. It was the first one of the afternoon." She fidgeted with her fleece zip as she spoke. "He was quiet. Kept to himself. I didn't really know him that well. But he wasn't usually one to exit a lecture early. Dean was very hard-working."

Dalgleish stepped forward, his tone gentle. "We understand this time will be difficult for you, but did you notice anything unusual in the past few days? Anyone coming or going from his room?"

The student hesitated, her gaze dropping to the floor. "I... I saw someone yesterday, but I don't know who. It was late, and they wore a hoodie, so I saw the back of them as they went into his room. I was on my way to the kitchen to make a milky drink. I don't think they were in there long... They had gone by the time I went back to bed."

"How did you know they had left?"

"I heard the door go at the end of the corridor, near the stairs, and Dean poked his head out, like he was checking they had gone. I said goodnight to him, but he didn't answer. He seemed preoccupied. He went back inside and closed the door. That was the last time I saw him. I carried on back to my room with my drink."

McKenzie exchanged a glance with Dalgleish. "Did you recognise anything about the hooded person? Any distinctive features?"

She shook her head. "No, it was dark. I was tired, and they were gone too quickly for me to register them properly. People are always coming and going here. And it's cold. Some people wear their hoods up."

McKenzie nodded, handing her a card. "Thank you for sharing this with us. It could be vital information. We may need to speak with you again."

"Sure." She bit her lip.

"And call us if you think of anything else you would like to share."

McKenzie noticed a tremor in her hands. "Is there something else?"

She swallowed hard. "I found this on the floor of my room this morning. I think it's his phone, but I can't be sure as I don't have the pin. But who else would have opened my door last night and placed it on the floor?"

McKenzie took the mobile from her with gloved hands. "Thank you. We'll take this." He placed it in an evidence bag. "You should lock your door at night."

She swallowed. "From now on, I will."

13

FOLLOW THE LEADER

Grant and Susan traversed the bustling streets of Edinburgh to the Eclipse, an exclusive nightclub with opulent décor and a reputation as a magnet for the city's elite. The sleek exterior belied that illicit activities might be happening beyond the glamorous façade.

The venue was quiet during the day, but Kenny Doyle, the nightclub's owner, visited the office on a Friday to speak to staff and go through the books, checking the week's takings and letting everyone know in no uncertain terms whether he was happy with their performance. It also gave him a chance to make certain they were ready for the weekend; the busiest and most lucrative time for the club.

Famous for running the establishment and a chain of gyms and spa complexes, Doyle had a reputation for ruling his growing empire with an iron hand. Few staff ever spoke out against him publicly, but private rumours were rife.

They spotted him at the bar; the centre of attention as he addressed a group of junior staff dressed to titillate rich patrons. Muscular and bullish, with wide shoulders and a shaved head, he exuded an air of arrogance and authority, appearing to revel in the power and attention he commanded. Approaching him, the detectives noted his grimace when he realised they were there.

"Kenny Doyle?" McKenzie held up his badge, his gaze piercing. "DI Grant McKenzie and this is DS Susan Robertson."

Doyle dismissed his staff with a wave of his hand; eyes narrowed. "Who are you looking for? I have things to do."

"We're here to speak with you," Robertson said, her tone direct. "We found your name in the back of a murder victim's notebook, and we are here to ask you why you think it was there."

Doyle's eyebrows shot up. "You come to my club to ask me about a murder? Is that how the police work now? Someone writes my name in their diary, because they have somehow heard about me, and you think I might have had them killed? Look around you. This is only one small part of my business. I have a worldwide reputation. People are going to have heard of me. Doesn't mean they know me at all. My name is probably in the back of many people's note-books... Most of them, female." His grin was a triumphant smirk, aimed at the DI. "People like me attract attention. It goes with the territory."

McKenzie inclined his head, pursing his lips. "That's a wee bit defensive, isn't it, Doyle? Jeezo... We haven't accused you of anything, Kenny. I think you need to calm down." The DI's gaze was steady as he noted the proprietor's chest rising and falling. What was he worried about?

Doyle leaned against the bar, crossing his arms. "Well, well. A murder victim's notebook, you say? That's a new one... How am I supposed to know why my name would be in some dead guy's book?"

The DI leaned in, his gaze unwavering. "You run high-profile businesses in this city. Nightclubs, gyms, spas... You're involved in a lot of things. So, let's not pretend you're clueless about the people who cross paths with you."

Doyle snorted. "You think I keep tabs on everyone who comes through my establishment doors? How much time do you think I have? Aren't you supposed to be out there fighting criminals? Not hassling top business men like me? I've got better things to be getting on with."

The DI glanced around at the long, well-stocked bar, and three large screens set above it at the back. "Are those for your CCTV?"

"They can be... They have multiple functions. Why do you want to know?"

"Do you know a man called Mark Anderson?"

Doyle gave a slow double-blink. "Can't say that I do."

"He seemed to know you."

"Och, so he's the laddie who wrote my name in his book, eh? I was probably his hero." He shrugged. "I can't say I blame him."

"How did you know he was young?"

"Eh?"

"You said, 'laddie'"

"It's just an expression."

"Have you seen the news lately? I mean, a businessman like you... You'd be following current events, wouldn't you?"

"Aye, I keep abreast of things."

"Then you would know about the body found on Arthur's Seat?"

Doyle placed his hands on his hips. "Are you accusing me of having something to do with that?"

"We think you're involved in much more than running clubs and gyms," Robertson chimed in, her tone cutting through Doyle's facade, "And we're not the only ones who've noticed." She flicked her head towards the young women he had been addressing when the detectives walked in. "How many girls have you got working for you?"

He narrowed his eyes. "A few..."

"Do they all work here at the club? Or do some work from home?" The DS looked up at the screens. "What else do you see on those?"

Doyle swallowed. "Nothing criminal, so it's none of your business."

"Was Anderson paying to watch content provided by your organisation?"

The bravado wavered, a fleeting expression of discomfort crossing the man's face before he regained composure. "I don't know what you're talking about. And if you've got nothing else, I suggest you leave."

McKenzie leaned his elbow on the bar, his voice a low warning. "We're watching you, Kenny. Keep that in mind."

With a dismissive wave, Doyle turned away from them, returning to his posse of admirers and junior staff.

As the detectives left the nightclub, McKenzie felt they hadn't even scratched the surface of what was going on behind those doors.

THEIR NEXT STOP was the Fairway Haven, a prestigious golf complex on the outskirts of Edinburgh, whose sprawling greens and manicured fairways attracted players from all over the world. The idyllic backdrop was at odds with the tension they felt as they travelled from the city centre after meeting Kenny Doyle.

Shaun McNeil, the enigmatic figure behind a resort

chain rumoured to house both legal and illegal gambling operations, awaited them in the clubhouse.

As the detectives approached, they couldn't ignore the unease radiating from the staff they encountered. It wasn't so much what people said; it was more their shyness, and a refusal to acknowledge the police officers' presence. They passed caddies who kept their eyes on the ground, and bartenders who looked the other way whilst their patrons stared at the officers out of curiosity. It raised the hairs on DS Robertson's back.

McNeil stood by two enormous windows overlooking the course, his demeanour aloof and guarded, an air of authority which hinted at the control he had over the establishment and the people within. His eyes were as sharp as his neatly trimmed grey hair and beard, adding to an imposing presence. He wore a tailored suit, cut for a lean body, in a multicoloured geometric pattern of red, black, and grey. Someone had embroidered his surname on the sunflower-yellow tie. The tension in his muscles showed an undercurrent of simmering annoyance, barely contained.

"Mr McNeil?" The DI held up his badge. "DI Grant McKenzie, and this is DS Susan Robertson."

McNeil regarded them, an eyebrow raised. "Officers, to what do I owe this pleasure?"

Robertson cast her eyes around the clubhouse. "Is there somewhere we can go?"

McNeil's lips curled into a tight smile. "I hope this won't take too long... I'm a busy man."

"We'll be brief," McKenzie assured. He got the feeling McNeil wanted them unsettled, to have the upper hand.

DS Robertson took out her notepad. "An informant tells us your resorts are being used for illegal gambling nights. Care to comment on that?"

McNeil's dark eyes bored into hers, his voice cool and measured. "I run legitimate businesses, Detective. Any allegations to the contrary are baseless, and probably propagated by my rivals... Of which there are many."

McKenzie exchanged a glance with Robertson. Both suspected the man's nonchalance masked something deeper. "Your employees seem uneasy around you." The DI kept his gaze level; his tone pointed.

McNeil's jaw tightened. "I expect a certain level of professionalism from my staff. Fear is an effective motivator. I won't get the best from them if they do not respect me. They put a foot out of line? I fire them. They know this, and it keeps them on their toes. I don't believe in prolonging an employment where the work ethic is poor. There is no probation period here. If my staff do not perform, they are out."

McKenzie cleared his throat. "We believe you have information relevant to an ongoing investigation... A murder inquiry."

McNeil's eyes flickered. A wave of uncertainty rippled across his features. "I assure you, officers, I wouldn't know anything *about* that. I don't think I can help."

"We have a photograph..." Robertson took one from her bag. "That's him... He was twenty-four years old."

McNeil glanced at the photo and shrugged. "I'm afraid I can't recall every individual I come across. I see many faces in my line of work."

McKenzie took a step forward. "This wasn't any individual, Mr McNeil. The young man's name was Mark Anderson."

"Never heard of him."

"He wrote your name in the back of his notebook. Why would he do that?"

McNeil shifted in his seat. "I do not know... You cannot hold me accountable for every fan or wannabe business-man. When you are successful, young men want to be like you. I'm a role model."

"We believe he owed someone money. We suspect the creditor had him killed because of the amount he owed or because Anderson knew too much."

"What has that got to do with me?"

"We think the debt was down to gambling and watching girls on webcams. We've found traces of both activities on his mobile phone."

McNeil frowned. "That was careless... The killer leaving evidence like that."

"Believe me, the murderers did their level best to wipe the device. But we have some of the best forensic techs in the business."

McNeil turned his face to the window and the golf course. Heavy rain had begun lashing the glass. "Maybe the girls had him killed?" He sneered. "Perhaps they killed him themselves?"

DS Robertson pressed him, her voice measured. "You maintain a tight grip on your businesses, yet you claim igno-rance of the gambling going on in your own establishments?"

McNeil brushed the thighs of his trousers as though removing breadcrumbs. "My focus is on the bigger picture. I can't micro-manage every employee. I can't be at every establishment twenty-four-seven."

"I thought you fired anyone who stepped out of line?"

"I do, when I know about it."

McKenzie rubbed his chin. "The murder victim's poten-tial connection to you, or knowledge of you, raises ques-tions. Surely, you understand that?"

McNeil turned abruptly, his composure reinstated. "I've told you everything I can. If that will be all I have other matters to attend to."

The DI glanced at his watch. "We will leave, for now... But I want you to think about what we have said. We will *probably* speak with you again."

"As you wish." McNeil walked away, the detectives exchanging a knowing glance. The encounter had ended, but the usually confident McNeil had looked uncomfortable. The man knew a lot more than he was saying.

IN THEIR CRAMPED office at the Leith police station, DC Dalgleish was at his desk, face illuminated by the glow of the computer screen. He turned to McKenzie, his expression serious. "Grant, I've been going through Goose's social media accounts, and I've stumbled upon something I think you should look at."

The DI crossed the room to Graham's desk. "What have you got?"

Dalgleish brought up a list of transactions on the screen. "Records showing sizeable sums of money paid to an anonymous organisation. The payments were made through an encrypted app, making it hard to trace the receiving party."

McKenzie studied the list. "An elusive organisation, eh? Any idea when we'll have the identity of the outfit?"

Dalgleish shook his head. "Not yet, but I'm working closely with the NCA; following the money trail to determine who the ultimate beneficiary is."

McKenzie's brow furrowed. "What's the connection to Goose?"

"Several of the payments were labelled 'Shania-M', sir."

Dalgleish sat back. "But the money didn't go to Shania McInnes's account."

McKenzie rubbed his forehead. "Was someone else using her name?"

"It seems likely the funds were monies she had earned for the company. If they are running several girls, they must have a system for keeping track of the amount each girl earns. That way, if one of them is not bringing in enough money, they can tell her to work harder or get rid of her. I'm guessing the women get paid a cut of whatever they bring in."

"I say we go to Shania again, and ask her for names."

"We could try, but here's the thing—She is afraid, and not talking. The firm has probably threatened her. These gangs warn their victims they will harm not only them but also their families. That's usually the way it goes, isn't it? They coerce girls into making content for viewers, even when they no longer want to. If the girl is popular, the firm won't let her leave."

"Unfortunately..." The DI grimaced.

"The clients dote on the women, but the girls do not bond with their viewers because there are hundreds, if not thousands, of them. And the firm almost certainly discourages fraternising with paying customers. She may have known Gordon was a fan, but not become familiar with him in any genuine sense. And could not have had a relationship with him. Remember, the gang knows the names and addresses, and a lot else besides, of these men. They would be a no-go area for the women."

McKenzie's fingers tapped rhythmically on the desk as he thought about it. "I think Shania may know what happened to Goose. I'll speak to the DCI... If McInnes wants out of working for this firm, we could offer her a place in Witness Protection."

Dalgleish nodded. "You could try her with that. In the meantime, I will continue working with the NCA to decrypt the money trail. It could get us to the heart of whatever Goose was involved in."

McKenzie pushed his hands into his pockets, his mind racing. "I will talk to her again. Find out what she knows, who she's afraid of, and if she wants out of it. We should approach this with care. Her safety is a priority. If she's being threatened, we should protect her as soon as possible, and get the information we need."

14

FAKE PERSONAS

McKenzie placed a mug of hot tea on Dalgleish's desk. "There you go... That's so you don't go telling anyone I never make the tea."

Dalgleish grinned. "I wanted to speak to you, anyway... I have information from our forensic bods and the NCA regarding Dean Mitchell's suicide."

"Go on..." McKenzie set down the tray loaded with several mugs waiting to be doled out and perched on the edge of the DC's desk.

"The findings from Dean's phone are quite telling, actually. There were exchanges between him and someone posing as a young woman. The messages escalated in intimacy, and Dean shared explicit photographs and videos with this supposed woman over a period of months. The true identity of this female was far from the created persona."

The DI frowned. "What did forensics reveal?"

"It turns out the messages didn't come from a woman at all. They originated from a male who has since gone off grid. This faker created multiple online personalities, male and female. The purpose behind them was to exploit vulnerable young men, straight and gay, into giving him money."

"Stolen identities?"

"He used profile photos nicked from social media to construct the fake IDs and catfish youngsters, all under the guise of offering companionship. He persuaded each victim to share compromising photos. And, once he had enough material, the fake companion dropped the act and explained he wanted money or the victim's friends and family would see the photos and videos."

"Jeezo, that scam has been doing the rounds."

"Dean Mitchell complied with the demands of the scammer, but the criminal kept asking for more."

"Chilling..."

"In the end, Mitchell was all out of funds. He took his own life, thinking everyone he cared about was about to see his explicit images. He believed his world was about to collapse."

"And he didn't have the life experience to see that today's news is tomorrow's chip paper."

Dalgleish nodded. "These schemes are sinister. The faker demanded substantial sums of money, all the while leveraging the Dean's fear of a tarnished reputation and personal life if he didn't comply. Mitchell would have felt cornered. He obviously saw suicide as his only way out."

"How soon can we have the scammer in here?"

"We have to catch him first... Like I say, he's gone to ground, and hasn't used his cell phone since. He's probably gotten rid of it by now. All photos shared from that pay-as-you-go device were someone else's. We don't have a lot to go on, as it stands."

"Could this extortion racket relate to Goose's abduction and Anderson's murder, I wonder?"

"Well, if the same gang is behind it all, it's possible. It is a hell of a coincidence that this happening at the same time."

"Are the NCA looking into this?"

"Aye, sir, they are. They think it is most likely a local criminal gang that will be involved in other cybercrimes and extortion rackets."

"The sooner we stop them, the better. It's not only about justice for Dean. There'll be other victims. The last thing we want is more suicides."

"Agreed." Dalgleish nodded towards the tray on his desk. "You had better give the others their tea or they'll be cursing you because it's gone cold."

McKenzie laughed. "It's okay... I got this."

THE DI KNEW he had to confront Shania. Lives were at stake, possibly including her own, and her involvement with a criminal enterprise couldn't be ignored any longer. She had to know that he knew.

As he entered the ambient Last Drop pub, Shania's gaze met his, a mix of defiance and uncertainty in her eyes. Her bobbed hair was up in a rough ponytail while she dried glasses, placing them on the shelving below the counter. The errant locks escaping from the hairband gave her a harried air. She flicked a glance around. It was still early, and they were alone.

"Sit down, Shania," Grant ordered, taking a seat at the bar across from her.

She hesitated before complying, her fingers tapping the countertop.

"I have something important to discuss with you," He kept his tone even. "I know you've been conducting webcam sessions to extract money from men."

Shania's jaw dropped. "I... I don't know what you're talking about."

Grant put both elbows on the counter, his eyes locking onto hers. "I know there must be more to the story, Shania. Most of the money you've earned hasn't made its way into your bank account. There's someone higher up the food chain, isn't there? Someone getting the lion's share? I think it's about time you started talking. We're dealing not just with murder, but with suicides of men who are being blackmailed."

A flicker of unease crossed her young features. "I'm not involved in anything like that."

Grant's gaze didn't waver. "You may not be... But the gang who are running the show, exploiting you and the other girls, are... they've got their grubby little claws in all sorts."

She swallowed.

"Now, let's talk about Gordon, my nephew. Where is he, and who is behind his abduction?"

Shania's eyes darted away, her whole body tensed. "I've already told you. I know nothing about that."

"Who do you answer to in the organisation?" The DI persisted.

Shania looked down at the counter.

"Why was Gordon taken?"

She folded her arms across her chest, leaning back and looking towards the door.

"Who's the puppet master, Shania? Who's pulling the strings?"

Her shoulders slumped, a mixture of anxiety and resignation clouding her features. "You have no idea what kind of danger you're getting us all into. I can't say anything. These people don't mess about..."

Grant leaned back, assessing her carefully. "You might think silence is your best option, but I can guarantee you it isn't."

"Tell that to the friends of Sheryl O'Farrell."

"Who?"

"Look her up... You'll find she went missing two years ago. Only, I don't think she lived much beyond a few days after they snatched her. She had no family, and had been a streetwalker before they saw her and pulled her into the business. She joined before I did, so I knew her only briefly. But she knew people, and she talked. They shut her up... Literally."

"I'll look into it... So, you met her?"

"Sure... They sometimes get two or more of us together for the men who want interaction."

"I see..."

"You need to know, I don't take my clothes off. Some do, I don't. Luckily, not everyone wants that. Some guys simply want someone to talk to. Imagine that? Paying crazy sums of money only to talk to someone. What a world we live in, eh?"

"What about the people running the show? Have you met them?"

"Oh, sure... I mean, that's how they rope you in. They don't tell you, at first, you're going to be on camera. They buy you meals; shower you with gifts; say you're the most beautiful girl they ever met and make you fall for them."

"And then what?"

She glanced at the door, biting her lower lip. "Then they tell you can make money with them. That the two of you will be wealthy if you do a bit of smiling into a camera."

"So tell me who they are?"

"I can't..."

"Remember that girl you think they murdered? The situation extends beyond you now... Others may suffer the same fate if we do not stop them. You can help us do that. We can protect you."

A shudder passed through Shania. Her fingers trembled where they lay on the bar. "I can't risk my life. You don't understand... They hear everything. They got Gordon's details from the conversations he had with me. The gang is well-informed about everything. They watch it all. Everything the men say; where they live; how much they can afford to pay. And they suck them dry using us girls. They tell us how to dress, and how to behave in front of the camera. They end up knowing the clients better than they know themselves, and they know exactly what we should do to get more money out of them. And they knew Gordon's uncle was a big fish in MIT because your nephew told me on web cam. I pulled a face at him as a warning, but he kept talking. I couldn't tell him to stop. That's not allowed. They would have punished me for that. And they don't know... the men... They think it is just them and me. They don't realise there is a gang out there watching and choreographing everything that happens."

Grant's gaze softened, his voice low with empathy. "Your safety is hanging by a thread, Shania. Cooperation might be your only lifeline. How long until you end up like Sheryl? How will you step out of line? Do you even know where the lines are? The ones you must not cross? And what if the rules change without warning? Can you ever feel safe? Are you really benefitting enough to justify the risks you are taking not only with your own safety, but with that of those you love?"

Shania sighed, her gaze dropping to her lap. After several seconds, she whispered, "Sheryl suffered because she wanted to speak up."

He inclined his head. "Do you know what happened to her? Do you know where she is? Where her body is?"

She shook her head.

McKenzie leaned back. A customer had come into the tavern. "Think about it," he said, sliding his card across the counter. "Call me if you change your mind."

15

SERENITY OF THE LAKE

After leaving St Margaret's Loch, McKenzie returned to his car as a heavy mist enveloped him and hovered over the water. The usual ambient sounds were eerily absent, leaving an unsettling quiet in the air. As he approached his vehicle, something caught his eye under the windscreen wiper.

A shiver ran the length of his spine as he reached for the envelope. The ominous feeling it invoked clenched his gut. He turned it over in his hands. There was no addressee on the outside. Tearing it open, the DI pulled out a laser-printed note. His eyes scanned the message, the words thrown like punches. He was being told to step away from the case or face the consequences. The lives of those he cared about, especially his nephew, were on the line if he didn't.

His grip on the paper tightened as frustrated anger welled in his chest. McKenzie cast his eyes around. Was the bearer of the note still present? Were they watching for his reaction? He refused to be intimidated, but the safety of his family was more important to him than anything else.

He climbed into his car, head spinning as though the mist itself had seeped into his mind, creating a haze that mired his thoughts and muddied the way forward.

Later, at the Leith police station, he handed the threatening missive to his team before sending it for forensic examination. The atmosphere in the office was tense as they read it, one-by-one.

"Make sure they process this as a priority," he instructed Helen McAllister, his voice a mixture of authority and angst. "We must trace where this came from. The writer of this letter knows about our investigation. And they almost certainly know where Gordon is, and what's happened to him. It must have come from the gang we are looking for."

Dalgleish nodded. "Aye, it looks like they are watching every move you make. You'll have to mention this to Sinclair, eh?"

McKenzie sighed. "Aye, and he won't be happy..." He ran a hand through ragged hair. "He'll want me off the case." McKenzie's thoughts turned to his nephew and the dangerous situation entangling them both. The quiet stillness of St Margaret's Loch seemed a distant memory, replaced by a storm threatening everyone he cared about.

~

McKenzie sat alone by the fire, the house finally quiet after putting his three children to bed. The weight of the ultimatum weighed heavily on his mind, and he knew he ought to share it with his wife.

Jane entered the room, a mug of tea in each hand. "I thought you could use this," she said, handing him one.

"Thanks..." His smile was fleeting.

"Is everything all right, Grant?" she asked, her brow furrowed in concern. "You're not yourself."

He sighed, motioning for her to sit beside him on the couch. "There's something I need to tell you," he began, his eyes studying her face. "I received a threat today... It's connected to Goose, and whatever he has gotten himself into."

"What kind of threat? Who threatened you?" Jane's eyes widened. "Are you in danger?"

He recounted the contents of the note, watching as his wife's expression shifted from concern to alarm. "They're demanding I back off from the investigation, or they'll harm Gordon and others I care about..."

Jane's hand instinctively reached for his, their fingers entwining. "This is... What are you going to do? Are they a threat to our children?"

The DI leaned back against the couch, his gaze fixed on the ceiling. He let out a heavy breath. "I don't know, my love. I can't bear the thought of anything happening to our kids. And Goose? Well, he is like a son to me, and he's already been through so much. It's left me in a ridiculous quandary. But, if I walk away from this case now? They win, don't they?"

"Have you told anyone about this? Have you spoken to Davina? Or the DCI?" Jane asked softly.

He shook his head. "Not yet... I've been agonising over it all. I know I need to do the right thing, but I can't shake the feeling that telling the DCI could put Goose in even more danger."

Jane's grip on his hand tightened. "You're a brilliant and dedicated police officer, love. But you're also human, and you're caught in an impossible situation. You can't face this alone. Speak to your DCI. Put the decision on his shoulders. It's what he's paid for. Don't carry this alone."

"What about you and the children? I don't want harm coming to any of you."

"I'll take the kids to mum's. She'll put us up for a couple of weeks while you sort things here. I know you'll want to carry on with this case and bring Goose home. I know you couldn't live with yourself if you didn't. But I will want to know that, when I return, my husband and my children's father will still be with us, and unharmed."

He took her in his arms. "Have I told you how amazing you are? You always seem to understand what I am going through and know the right thing to do. What would I do without you?"

"Well, if I go to mother's for a couple of weeks, you'll find out..." She pulled a face. "But seriously, you stay in one piece, okay? If I take the kids, it is so you can do your job without fear of reprisals on us. But I will be worried sick about you. So you phone and text me every day, you hear? Don't leave me guessing, Grant."

"I'll phone and text every day, and say goodnight to the kids," he affirmed. "I will miss you all like hell."

"And speak to Sinclair?"

McKenzie nodded, his thoughts a mess of conflicting emotions. "I have to do what's right, even if it means risking my career or worse. But I have to buy time, gather more information. If there's a chance I can protect Goose without endangering him further, I must take it. I am worried that if I go to Sinclair now, he will take me off the case."

"Would that be so bad?" She inclined her head.

"Look, I don't know what Gordon has gotten himself into, or even if he is involved with this gang. I know I shouldn't, but I worry he might have had a hand in Mark Anderson's murder. I mean, I can't imagine Goose doing anything like that, but he had an argument with Anderson in the street only days before the killing. God... What a mess."

Jane leaned her head on his shoulder, a gesture of comfort and understanding. "You're not alone in this, my darling. We'll figure it out together. I may be miles away at my mother's, but I will only be a phone call or text from you. Don't shut me out. Don't go through this on your own."

"I won't..."

"Promise?"

"Promise."

AS THE NIGHT WORE ON, Grant's inner turmoil persisted. Sleep remained elusive for hours, his mind fighting a battle between duty and family. He stared at the ceiling, grappling with the weight of everything, until his eyelids became irresistibly leaden, and he finally succumbed to sleep.

16

CRIMINAL HOLDINGS

The tight-lipped figure, the gang referred to by the sobriquet, The Man, leaned back in his chair in a room lit via two table lamps. Fingers steepled beneath his chin; eyes steely and calculating, he waited for the messenger to confirm his note had been found and read. "Well?" The gruff voice demanded immediate answers.

The young male swallowed hard. "Aye, I saw him take the envelope from under the windscreen wiper. He had it in his hand."

"But did he open it? And did he read it?" The Man leaned forward, bringing his fist down on the table. "Don't keep me waiting, lad."

"Aye, aye, he read it."

"You saw him?"

"Yes, I was watching from behind parked vehicles. He read it."

"Did he see you?"

"No, definitely not, though he was looking about. He seemed mad as hell. I think if he could have got his hands on me, he'd have killed me right there and then."

A young woman brought a metal tray to the table, placing a double whisky in front of The Man. She swallowed, careful not to look at the messenger, just as he was careful not to look at her. They kept their eyes on the table as she withdrew. Both were pawns in a game controlled by the moody man in front of them, his face obscured by the blinding lights.

He swilled his whisky around the glass, ice chinking against its sides. "You know what's at stake here?" he asked, his voice devoid of emotion, but carrying a chill that made them shiver. "Your families, your loved ones, are all vulnerable. I trust you understand the depth of that vulnerability. If anyone asks questions, you keep your mouths shut."

The girl swallowed hard, and the messenger nodded. Though they didn't speak, their acquiescence was clear from their cowed demeanour.

The Man leaned forward, his aura of menace palpable. "Good, because if anyone even thinks about speaking out, well... let's say your families won't sleep peacefully again." He sat back, the venomous promise left hanging in the air.

The girl shook, like his words had a tightened a noose around her throat; the air in the room was suffocating.

He dismissed them both with a wave of his hand, his gaze shifting to the enforcers — loyal, ruthless bodyguards who stood ready to do whatever he asked of them.

"Lads," he said with a sinister smile, looking up at the bank of screens on the wall, each displaying a live feed from young women communicating with their clients, "keep your eyes on those girls. If there is a weak link among them, I want to know about it. Make sure they only do what they are supposed to."

∾

McKenzie sat across from DS Susan Robertson in the main office at Leith Police Station. The room was silent save for the sound of tapping on keyboards in the background as they delved into the case of Sheryl O'Farrell.

Grant's fingers drummed lightly on the table, his gaze fixed on the file spread before them. "You know, Sue," Grant began, his tone thoughtful, "Sheryl O'Farrell's disappearance baffled CID from the start. Eighteen months, gone without a trace, and still no leads. But they suspected she left under her own steam. They weren't looking at this as a murder..."

"Right... If they had thought her deceased, the case would have come to us." Susan nodded, her brow furrowing. "It's a puzzling one, Grant. I'm surprised they shelved the case so quickly. And no-one found her body."

"It looks to me like they did not know she was involved in webcam work. No-one mentioned it as a possibility to the investigating officers."

"I think that alone tells us how tight a grip this gang has on the people it controls."

The DI leaned back, exhaling. "I've been looking into the details again. Shania McInnes has all but admitted she is in too deep with the gang. I think she is terrified of them."

"Well, if she is right about what happened to Sheryl, who can blame her? Do you think she will talk to you again? Does she know where her friend's remains are?" Susan pursed her lips, her gaze intense. "What did she tell you?"

"According to Shania, whether they were involved directly, the gang is connected to the woman's disappearance." McKenzie smoothed his beard. "She implied Sheryl talked too much for the gang's liking. She thinks they killed O'Farrell because of it, but claims not to know what they did with her."

Susan frowned. "What if O'Farrell ran away to escape the gang? Do you really believe she was trying to expose them and they murdered her for it? Or could Shania be wrong about Sheryl's fate?"

"It's possible," Grant agreed. "Although McInnes thought it was more to do with Sheryl talking about the gang and their activities to friends. She was letting things slip, she was actively discussing them. The gang doesn't want the law, or the public, to know anything at all. Only the girls know the truth. They use the 'lover-boy method' to lure them in."

Susan tapped her pen on the table. "We should monitor the young women's movements; find out where they go and who they see. The boss or bosses have to contact them somehow."

Grant nodded. "Agreed. We'll dig into it; look for patterns and associations."

"We could start with financial transactions and communications. They are some of the most difficult things to hide, especially when the girls only have one bank account... Unless they are laundering cash for the gang."

McKenzie nodded. "The whole shebang revolves around money, but I think they are using payment apps. They'll be concocting fake purchases to cover themselves. But the money trail is where we will find the answers." Susan looked over at Dalgleish. "And Graham is the man for that..."

The DI leaned forward, a determined glint in his eyes. "We owe it to Sheryl and Shania to uncover the truth, and that means taking on this gang and risking the consequences."

Susan met his gaze, her head cocked. "What about your nephew?"

He sighed. "I think they took him as insurance to keep

me off their case. Don't you? If I get too close, they threaten to harm or kill him. If I am right, they will hold Goose somewhere close by. Probably in a safe house. We have to find out where, and get him out of their grasp *before* we take them down."

17

MAPPING CRIME

In the eerie ambience of a mist-shrouded Edinburgh Castle, DI McKenzie and Jock Munro met at the edge of the gravel car park. The place was awash with tourists and vehicles, but provided an ideal place to melt into the background, away from the city centre. Grant thought it better they meet somewhere neutral, wary of the gang watching for his every move. The last thing he wanted was to put Gordon's best friend at risk.

The air was frigid; an icy breath that seeped into bones. McKenzie buttoned his black wool overcoat, turning the collar up against the chill. His every exhalation hung like a vaporous veil in the air, mingling with the swirling mist that clung to the ancient stones like a cloak.

Jock Munro exuded a palpable unease that radiated from his rigid posture and nervous head swings. His bomber jacket and tight jeans were an inadequate shield against the numbing air. He shivered, pushing his hands into the pockets of his jeans to warm them against his thighs. Perhaps the cold was not the only thing causing him to shake. Maybe the weight of what he knew added to the jitters. His darting eyes betrayed anxiety, as if the mist-laden landscape held some hidden threat.

McKenzie's gaze remained steadfast, piercing the mist and unease. His patience waning thin, he charged the atmosphere with an unspoken tension, convinced the lad knew more than he was saying. "Jock," His voice cut through the mist like a blade. "We can't dance around this any longer. Gordon's connections; his conversations... Everything matters if we are to find him. You don't want Goose ending up like Anderson, do you? Up there, on Arthur's Seat?"

"No... No, of course I don't." The boy's eyes wandered nervously around the castle grounds, his breathing shallow and rapid. He cleared his throat, shifting the weight between his feet; lips quivering. "I-I've told you, Mr McKenzie," he answered. The voice was so quiet it was almost lost in the swirling mist, "I don't know what happened to Goose. All I know is he disappeared from outside of the tavern."

"What was Gordon into before he vanished?" McKenzie's tone was firm. "Come on, you know something. I can see it. Speak, man... Tell me what he was up to."

Jock's shoulders tensed, another shiver wracking his body, the struggle between fear and responsibility palpable. "He was just being a lad like the rest of us. It could have been any of us that got taken."

"Was he talking to girls on the webcam?" McKenzie's gaze remained steady, the only clarity in their mist-ridden surroundings. "Do you webcam, too?"

Munro was silent, his eyes on the ground.

"Tell me about the girls, Jock, and the connection with Gordon."

The lad kicked a small stone across the car park. "Shania McInnes. She's one of them. He was talking to her."

"On webcam?"

"Aye..."

"For money?"

"Aye... He paid for her time, and whatever else she allowed."

"Was it only Shania, Jock? Or were there other girls?" The DI's gaze was earnest as he placed a hand on each of the lad's shoulders. "Was Gordon grabbed because he was talking to Shania? Or did Goose orchestrate his own disappearance as a cover for something else... like murder?"

"What?" Munro frowned. "How can you say that? He's your flesh and blood. Why would Goose have planned all this?"

Grant ran his hands through his hair, stepping back from Munro. "I don't know, but since you told me about the row he had with Anderson before his death, I've... I've had my doubts."

"Oh, I see... You think he ran because he had something to do with Mark Anderson's murder? What kind of uncle are you?" Munro spat the words. "And the killing happened after Gordon's disappearance, didn't it?"

"Tell me what Goose got himself mixed up with. Who had he pissed off, Jock? And why?"

Munro's gaze fell to the ground. He rubbed the back of his neck. "Sugar daddies, McKenzie. The girls have rich men paying for... stuff."

Grant frowned. "So, not the same men paying for webcam favours?"

"No... Not exactly... I mean, it's all linked, I guess. But it's complicated." He flicked his head around, checking there was no-one close enough to overhear. "There are men who pay online to talk to the women and get them to do things like dress a certain way, or do other stuff. All that depends on the girl, and how far she will go..."

"Go on..."

"Well, some of those women also have sugar daddies. They are the people in control. They get all the money coming in from the webcam clients. And, believe me, those sums can be huge. And they give some back to the girls. The women hang out with the rich guys, go to dinner, and whatever else they are prepared to do within the arrangement, in return for more of the money. Does that make sense?"

"How would that have affected Goose?" McKenzie frowned, trying to understand the link.

"Maybe he stepped on someone's toes. Those rich guys? They are possessive about their sugar babies. You know what I mean? If Goose was getting too involved, and trying to see a woman outside of the confines of the webcam, that would be a problem. And those sugar daddies don't mess around. They don't have that kind of patience."

"Would the girls know where Gordon is? Would Shania know?"

Jock shrugged. "She isn't talking. Those men expect total obedience from their women. They won't let them go once they are involved with the gang. They make it really difficult or even dangerous for the girls to leave."

McKenzie's brow furrowed. "Names, Jock. Give me names."

Munro's eyes flitted around. "Two of the names I've heard tossed around are Kenny Doyle and Shaun McNeil. They could be sugar daddies? I don't know if the rumours are true, but Gordon said that most of the rich men involved have several women each, not only one."

"Goose told you this?"

"He said something about it, yes. We'd been drinking, and he was talking about one girl in particular."

"Shania McInnes?"

Jock looked at his shoes. "Yes..."

"Do these men, or any of the gang, know that you have been told anything?"

"Not unless Gordon said something to them." He lifted round eyes back to the detective. "Do you think they will get it out of him? Ask him who he's talked to?"

The DI stared into the distance. "I don't know... It all depends what they think Gordon knows, and why they abducted him." He sighed. "I hope he doesn't run his mouth with them. I hope he keeps quiet about what he's heard."

"Me, too..." Jock swallowed hard.

"Goose must have gotten all this from talking to one woman." He turned back to Munro. "Who talked to Gordon about the gang? Was it Shania?"

"I don't know for sure. He didn't tell me, but I got the impression it was her. She is the one Goose has a thing for. He fancies her rotten. I also got the impression she wants out of the arrangement with the gang, but feels unable to escape the group's clutches. It would be dangerous for her to cross them... For her, and her family."

"Aye, she needs our help, but she's not asked me for it. She's too scared. Whatever you do, don't go mentioning to anyone that you've spoken to me. And I mean *anyone*."

"Are you going to get them all, Mr McKenzie?"

"Aye, if we can, we will take them all down."

Jock shivered. "I better go."

As the mist continued clinging to the ancient monument, Grant watched Munro set off through the car park and down the hill. He waited a further fifteen minutes before walking back to his vehicle.

SEVEN O'CLOCK IN THE EVENING, and the DI was still in the office at Leith police station. He and DC Dalgleish were alone, and hunched over a schematic they had drawn up with the names of men believed to be part of the gang, and the known associations with others. There were lots of gaps; things they didn't yet know. But they had enough to dig deeper.

"You think Shania will talk?" Dalgleish straightened, his eyes darting over the mind map.

"I don't know... Her knowledge would give us a head start, but I feel uncomfortable putting her in danger. I suspect they are watching her closely. And I have a feeling they are watching me."

"Aye, they know your vehicle, that's for sure."

"You ought to be getting home, Graham."

"So should you... Do you think Sinclair will take you off the case tomorrow?"

"I don't see that he'll have a choice."

"You don't have to tell him about the threat-"

"I can't hide something like that. If things went wrong, and it came out. It would be a disciplinary for sure, and maybe worse."

"But you can't work the case from home."

"I'll ask Sinclair to keep me on it, but if he refuses, it will be down to him and the rest of you. But that doesn't mean I can't ask questions as a citizen about the disappearance of my nephew."

"It's dodgy ground, that."

McKenzie grinned. "Tell me about it."

"What about Jane and the kids? You'll have to keep them safe."

"Jane has taken the children to her parents' home. Our house will be deadly quiet when I get back. I'm not looking forward to that."

"Och, you'll be making your own tea."

The DI grimaced. "I'll maybe get a takeaway."

THE DESK LAMPS cast long shadows around the room in step with the unease hovering over the DI. Exhaustion hazed his thoughts, a weariness reflecting the murk in the investigation. He knew the dangers of a waning rationality when the boundaries between duty and family blurred.

Dalgleish's voice broke through his thoughts. "Sir, I've been digging into the connections between several young women and some heavily cloaked accounts associated with offshore companies."

McKenzie's tired eyes met Graham's. "What have you found?"

The DC pointed to his notes. "I'm fairly sure the accounts belong to the sugar daddy types Munro told you about. It's probably more complex than that, but they are paying the girls."

"More complex, how?"

"They give them money and possessions in return for company and favours while also running them as webcam girls."

"Do we have evidence?"

"I'm working on it. They are experts at covering their tracks. The money trail is a minefield."

McKenzie nodded. "Keep on it. People are dying, and Goose is still missing. We need answers." The DI checked his watch. "But you need to get on home now. Go on... Off."

Graham grinned, grabbing his jacket. "I'm going... Remember to eat."

18

A WORLD AWAY

McKenzie parked his car in the driveway. The familiar sight of his quiet suburban home welcomed him back with security lights that lit up as he approached. His body cast a deep shadow across the lawn as he made his way inside, sighing at the sight of empty rooms instead of his wife and children. Not that the kids would have been up. They would have been in bed, though likely not yet sleeping. He wondered how they were getting on at Jane's parents' as he entered the solitude of his deserted home.

The silence weighed on him even as he kicked off his shoes. Jane would hand him a hot mug of something about now and ask him what he fancied to eat. The realisation he had taken it all for granted hit him like a swipe to the head. "I'm sorry, Jane," he whispered, wandering into the kitchen to put the kettle on.

He switched on the light and there, on the counter, propped up against a mug with a tea-bag already inside, was a note from his wife.

'I've made a shepherd's pie. It's in the fridge. Heat in the microwave. Call me when you can. We love you, Jane.'

It put an enormous grin on his face. He really didn't deserve her.

The food was delicious and warming. He felt better after and followed it with tea, pouring water on the bag his wife had thoughtfully placed in the mug hours before.

As he settled into an armchair, tv remote in hand, his phone rang. The caller ID displayed his sister's name. He picked up the phone with trepidation.

"Hello?"

"It's Davina," came her frantic voice. "How are you doing with my son's case? Gordon is still missing, and I'm losing my mind here. I cannot settle when I don't know where he is."

McKenzie's heart sank. He would have to tell his sister that, despite all his protestations, Sinclair would likely take him off the case the following day to avoid a conflict of interest.

"Davina," he said, carefully choosing his words, "I understand how you feel, but you know I can't officially work on this anymore. It's against the rules." He thought about telling her of the threat he received, but decided against worrying her further.

His sister's voice trembled on the other end of the line. "Grant, please, you're the only one I trust to do this. Can't you look into it unofficially? We're desperate..."

McKenzie closed his eyes, torn between his duty as a police officer and love for his family. He couldn't turn his back on his sister. But it would likely get him into all kinds of trouble.

"I'll see what I can do," he conceded, "but I make no promises."

He could hear the gratitude and relief in her voice. "Thank you... It means the world to me."

After the call, McKenzie ran both hands through his hair. How would he explain it to his sister if he could not follow through? Sinclair was no pushover. And the last thing the DI needed was a suspension from duty. And he missed his own family terribly. The empty house amplified his dilemma. To continue investigating Gordon's disappearance was to risk his family being hurt. But the alternative would hurt his sister and let Goose down.

Once again, he lay in bed tossing and turning, unable to find sleep, running everything around in his brain. He finally made a vow to himself. He would find a way to balance duty and family. His children deserved more of his time, and he would make sure they got it, even while he searched for his nephew. Having made that resolution, he drifted into slumber.

GRANT STEPPED into Sinclair's office as the winter sun streamed through the window at Leith police station. He loosened his tie, sweat beading on his brow. The DCI liked his radiator at maximum output, and McKenzie was already anxious. The resultant stress sent his sweat glands into overdrive. Grant glanced at the window and thought about opening it. He refrained. Sinclair appeared reluctant to look up from the paperwork stacked on his desk.

The DCI finally surfaced from the stack of case files in front of him, running a hand over his neatly combed, salt-and-pepper hair. He was in full uniform for an important meeting later that day. He raised both brows as the DI approached, eyes locking onto Grant's. "McKenzie," he began, his tone expectant. "How is it going?"

The DI hesitated for a moment, his hand closed over the folded letter in his pocket. Should he change his mind and not disclose it? His eyes crossed to the window once more. Could he simply ignore the missive? After all, any nut could have put the envelope under his windscreen window, couldn't they? What harm would it do to toss it into the bin? He chided himself for the thought. The stakes for such a move were far too high. "Sir, I've received a threatening letter. I thought you should know." He cleared his throat, producing the folded paper from his pocket and handing it to the DCI.

Sinclair's steely gaze shifted from McKenzie to the note. He unfurled it with deliberate care, turning it over in his hands, eyes scanning the laser-printed words. A furrow creased his brow. "This is a serious matter, Grant," he said, finally looking up from the missive. "You realise your involvement in this case must now be over. I can take it from here."

The DI's heart sank at the words he had known would come, but dreaded. He had worked tirelessly on the case, and it was being prised from his grasp. "But, sir," McKenzie began, his voice hoarse, "Shania has opened up. And she is only talking to me. I've made progress, and I can get more information. I know I can."

Sinclair leaned back in his chair, pursing his lips, expression unyielding. "I admire your dedication and tenacity, Grant, but this is procedure. You're too close to this, and your safety, and that of your family, is under threat. Your personal involvement could jeopardise the investigation. I know you are desperate to find your nephew. However, I think it is clouding your judgement."

McKenzie opened his mouth to remonstrate, but closed it again. He had known the rules, and Sinclair was right. Still, the disappointment was like a punch to the gut.

Sinclair continued, his tone softening. "Take some time off. Clear your head. We will sort this out, but for now, I want you to step back. Trust the rest of us to get on with it, and to do what is necessary."

"I'd like to continue working, if that is okay with you? There are other things to be getting on with, and I really don't want time off at the moment."

Sinclair nodded. "Very well, but you must abide by my instruction not to involve yourself in this case. And keep me abreast of what is happening with your family. We'll get protection for you if necessary."

As the DI left Sinclair's office, he felt wholly dejected. Not only was his family gone for the duration, but he couldn't even throw himself into the case. At least, not officially.

SHANIA MCINNES SAT in a dimly lit room, bathed in the cold, blue glow of a computer screen. Her hands trembled as she stared at the camera, knowing that unseen eyes watched her every move. It had been months since she had fallen into this twisted world, a place where fear and desperation ruled every decision.

The Man, a shadowy figure whose name sent shivers down her spine, loomed like a malevolent spectre. Even the thought of his presence suffocated her. Shania had seen what happened to those who defied him, and the consequences were too horrifying to contemplate. So she, like the other girls who had fallen into this nightmare, carried on against her own best judgement.

She longed to escape the gang; to break free from the web of coercion ensnaring her. But The Man held her family's safety in a vice-like grip, a threat hanging over her like a thundercloud. He left her in no doubt that talking to the police would be a death sentence for her and her loved ones. And he had gang members watch her and the other girls. Grunts observing their every move, ready to report the moment they stepped out of line.

Tears welled in her eyes as she continued on the webcam, performing for the faceless clients on the other side of the screen. Every movement was a lie, a facade of falseness concealing the torment within her. She felt violated, degraded, and helpless.

As she forced a smile at the lens and danced around the room in a stupid outfit, her heart ached with despair. She was a prisoner in her own life, a puppet dancing on strings pulled by the malevolent puppeteer. The reality of her situation ground her down, suffocating any glimmer of hope she might have had. Her thoughts turned to McKenzie. Could he and his team really be the solution? Should she talk to him? Or would that be a risk too far?

19

CHAPERONES

Grant sat at his cluttered desk, frustrated at not having access to either his nephew's case, or that of Mark Anderson. The walls of his office had born witness to the occasional unsolved mystery, but this was different. This was personal, and the last thing he wanted was for it to end up on the cold case pile. The sound of voices prevented him from wallowing further.

DC Dalgleish and DS Robertson entered, deep in conversation; faces animated.

"Hey up, you two... What's going on?" he asked, feeling excluded.

"Grant," Dalgleish glanced around the room before continuing, his voice low. "Mark Anderson was at the Last Drop tavern on the night Goose was abducted."

McKenzie's eyes widened. "Was he?"

"He was. We've looked through hours of CCTV footage from that night, trying to piece together Anderson's movements during the last few days of his life. He was sitting at the end of the bar for a couple of hours. In that time, he only had one beer, and what appeared to be two glasses of coke."

The DI frowned. "Was he on his own?"

Susan nodded. "He was, but he had his eyes on Shania McInnes the whole time."

"For the whole two hours?"

"Virtually from the time he entered the place."

"Was he watching Gordon, too?"

Dalgleish shook his head. "He didn't seem to watch your nephew. His eyes were mostly on the girl."

McKenzie's heart quickened. "Anderson's presence at the Last Drop? That has to be more than coincidence." He frowned. "Shania's name was in his notebook."

"He was obviously crushing on her." Susan pulled a face. "He and Gordon must have been rivals."

The DI rubbed his forehead. "I know you shouldn't be discussing this with me, but what if Goose had something to do with Anderson's death?"

"They didn't acknowledge one another." Dalgleish pushed his hands into his trouser pockets. "Not once, during the two hours, did we see Gordon and Anderson even look at each other. Both watched Shania as she drank with her friends... Anderson, even more than Goose."

McKenzie leaned back in his chair, running a hand through his hair. "Well, since I am officially off the case," he said with a sigh. "You two need to inform Sinclair."

The weight of that statement hung in the air, depressing the mood. The DI had been the driving force behind the investigation. His removal left the team feeling unsure, almost rudderless. Sinclair had a more hands-off style of leadership. The DS and DC were unused to that kind of management.

"But," McKenzie continued, his voice resolute, "I'd like you to keep digging. Was Anderson watching Shania on other occasions? Cast the net wider; look at CCTV footage from a broader range of dates. Interview witnesses. What was Anderson's involvement in all this, and who wanted him out of the way?"

Dalgleish and Robertson nodded, their determination matching McKenzie's. They would uncover the truth about Gordon, for the DI, who couldn't do it himself. They were a team.

After the others had left for the day, Grant's thoughts turned to Shania, the young woman caught in the twisted web at the heart of the case. He had to talk to her again in the hope she could shed light on Anderson's motives. She was the route to unlocking the secrets of the gang. Shania McInnes could be the key to the whole shebang.

GRANT FOUND himself entrenched in a mire of information surrounding another case, but his mind refused to let go of the murder of Mark Anderson and the sinister abduction of his nephew Gordon. He ran his hands through his hair, frustrated with the situation, and nursing a throbbing headache.

DC Dalgleish entered the office; his forehead creased in thought.

"Are you okay, Graham?" McKenzie asked, sensing this would be no routine update.

Dalgleish checked the door behind him before answering. He cleared his throat. "I've been digging into Anderson's finances, trying to make sense of what was going on in his life...You won't believe what I've found."

McKenzie leaned his chin on his hands. "Go on..."

"He had thirty-thousand pounds in his bank account, Grant. Thirty-thousand pounds!"

"Thirty grand? Anderson? How was that even possible? We've seen his place, Graham. It was nothing but a rundown hovel with a bunch of clapped-out second-hand furniture. He lived like a pauper."

"Exactly."

"Why was he keeping such a low profile?"

"I know, right? And where did he get the dosh? Early twenties? Without a well-paid job? He doesn't have rich relatives. It had to be dirty money."

McKenzie nodded. "He must have been leading a double life—presenting as a person struggling to make ends meet while someone was evidently paying him sizeable sums." His thoughts raced. "What if Anderson was involved with the gang who abducted Gordon? The Gang behind the webcam business?"

Dalgleish pursed his lips. "You don't think he was doing webcam, do you? He was hardly a looker..." He pulled a face.

"Och, of course I don't... Jeezo..." McKenzie grinned. "But perhaps he was involved somehow? We know he was watching Shania, right?"

"Sure..."

"Well, what if it wasn't because he had a crush? What if it was his job?"

"Sort of like a chaperone or guard?" Dalgleish frowned.

"Right... A chaperone. Someone to make sure she didn't get up to anything with random men, and to make sure none of the punters attacked her."

"Hence the beef with Gordon?"

"Exactly... If Anderson's job was to fend off unwanted male attention from webcam girls such as Shania, he may have warned Goose off. Maybe that was the reason for the altercation in the street?"

The DC nodded. "It makes sense... Anderson's financial secrets, his connections to Shania and the Last Drop—it all points in that direction. He may very well have been working for the people who took Gordon."

"Good... I would ask you to keep me informed, but... Well, you know..." The DI sighed.

"Aye, I know... You're officially off the case." He winked. "I'm not telling you anything."

McKenzie grinned. "Good."

"Oh, there's something else..."

"Yes?"

"Anderson was in The Last Drop a lot. We have footage of him in there every night she was. And that included social and work-related instances. He didn't communicate with her once, that we could make out, but he was watching her. And my feeling is that she was aware, from her body language and frequent checking in his direction... Like she knew she had to behave when he was there."

"Did she look uncomfortable with him watching?"

"I'd say she looked nervous as hell."

"Poor girl."

"Aye, it's no life, eh?"

"How in the world did she get herself mixed up in it all?"

"Aye, and how many other young women have they dragged into the business?"

After Dalgleish left, the DI contemplated the potential significance. Mark Anderson, a man who lived a life of humble means, had a considerable sum stashed away in his bank account. His modest flat, furnished with hand-medowns and worn-out relics, painted a starkly contrasting picture of the man he presented to the world. And then there was the watching... Was Anderson working for the elusive mastermind behind the dubious webcam business?

Grant would go to see Shania McInnes again.

20

THE WATCHER

The bar of the Last Drop had quietened down and the orders for food had finished, for now.

McKenzie decided it was the right moment to approach the harried girl behind the bar.

Shania busied herself with washing and polishing glasses, unaware of the detective's approach.

"Shania?" He inclined his head. "May I speak with you?"

She frowned. "I thought we said all we had to say last time?" She cast her eyes about the establishment.

McKenzie wondered if a replacement chaperone lurked somewhere around. "I'm sorry... I won't take up much of your time. It's just... My nephew is still missing. I'll keep my voice low. Let me know if someone is watching you. I'll make sure they can't read my lips."

She sighed. "What is it?"

"Mark Anderson."

She swallowed. Sweat beading on her upper lip.

McKenzie continued. "My nephew had an altercation with Anderson days before he disappeared. And later, Anderson was murdered."

Her shoulders relaxed, relief palpable. "Oh well, I wouldn't know anything about that." She continued polishing.

"He was watching you, wasn't he?"

She stopped cleaning. Eyes on the pint glass in her hand.

"He was in here virtually every day, wasn't he?"

Her shoulders tensed.

"Shania?"

"What are you doing here?" She hissed at him. "What do you want me to say?"

"I know, that you know, he was watching you."

She swallowed.

"He was working for them, wasn't he?"

Her eyes were back on the glass. She shrank into herself, becoming smaller; vulnerable, her shoulders rounded.

"They were paying him to make sure you didn't step out of line. Am I right?"

No answer.

"Shania? I'd like to help you."

"You can help by leaving me alone."

"I think you'd like to escape the trap you have gotten yourself into. And I bet there are dozens more like you. Women who find themselves in over their heads."

She lifted soulful eyes to his. Tears glistened inside them. "You don't know these men." She flicked a quick look around again. "You have no idea what they are capable of."

"I think I do, actually..." He grimaced. "I have bodies, and missing nephew as pointers."

She mopped her lip and ran a hand through her hair. "I can't talk to you here."

"Then where?"

She flicked her eyes to the door, where a group of men were chatting.

Grant recognised Goose's friend Jock, and waved.

Munro waved back before making his way towards the DI.

McKenzie turned back to Shania, but she had disappeared back behind the bar, pulling pints for two punters who were waiting.

She kept her eyes on the filling glasses, and did not look at Grant again.

"Hey, Mr McKenzie... Any news of Gordon?" Jock inclined his head.

"No, I'm afraid not." Grant sighed. "I was hoping you might have some news for me."

Munro shook his head. "Nah, sorry, I haven't heard a thing. It must be worrying for you and the family."

McKenzie nodded. "His mum is beside herself."

"Aye well, I'll keep my ear to the ground then, eh?"

"Aye, you do that." McKenzie turned his attention back to Shania, but she studiously avoided his gaze.

The detective decided not to force the issue when she was busy. He turned on his heel and left the tavern.

∾

"For Christ's sake!" The Man roared across the room. "I thought we made it clear. We obviously didn't make it plain enough. The bastard keeps coming back. Will he not learn? McKenzie shouldn't be anywhere near this case. He's got skin in the game. He shouldn't be involved. What are his superiors thinking?" He brought his fist down on the table. Several drinks splashed the counter as the glasses bounced.

The room was pitch-black save for those around the table

who sat wide-eyed in the light coming from the lamps, like inter-rogation subjects, except no-one dared speak. The Man was angry. Anything could happen.

"And you! Where the hell were you?" He spat the words at the young lad, who dared not move a muscle.

"I was there, like I was supposed to be-"

"Well, didn't you say something?"

"I have to be careful, don't I? I can't give the game away. You would nae want that, would you? He suspects everything. I didn't want him tracking me back to you."

"You're fucking useless, the lot of you." He swung around, his brow creased; eyes like lasers. "And you? What is it with you?"

Shania swallowed.

"Why is he showing such an interest in you? Eh? Have you been talking?"

"No-"

"Aye, I bet you have. You girls are a liability. Pity I don't have a business without you, eh? But, if I find out you've been running your mouths, it'll be the last time... You know what I'm saying..."

Shania kept her eyes on the floor, her thoughts turning to the unexpected visit from the DI.

"Is he interested in you?"

She shook her head.

"Aye well, maybe you should work on that, eh? Get him inter-ested. He's got a wife and kids, eh? Maybe you could move your useless ass and get him going, so we can have leverage. Now that would be a useful bit of work for you. If we can't buy him, we could blackmail him."

"I think his family has moved out." The young lad lifted his face, sure this piece of information would win kudos.

"What?" The Man frowned.

"Aye, they packed a few bags..."

"His wife and kids?"

"Aye."

"Well, where've they gone?"

The lad shrugged. "I dunno."

"Well, didn't you follow them?"

"I wasn't in a car."

"Like I said, you're fucking useless. You only give me half the story, eh? What do I pay you for? Maybe I should stop paying you?"

The lad opened his mouth, but closed it again. Eyes on the floor once more. The threat rang in his ears, a reminder of the precarious nature of both his employment and personal safety.

Shania watched the exchange, torn between the need for payment from The Man and moral reservations. She knew agreeing to entrap the DI would lead her down a dark and precarious path from which there might be no return. The weight of the proposal pressed on her as she weighed options.

After a long pause, she finally spoke, her voice trembling as her eyes glassed over. "All right... I'll do it... I'll get close to him. But you must promise me that no harm will come to his family."

The Man's bitter smile sent a chill down her spine. "Don't worry, bonny lass... We'll take care of everything. Just remember who you are, and why you earn what you do. And remember... there's no turning back now."

21

FEMME FATALE

G rant's phone buzzed on the kitchen counter. "DI McKenzie..." He frowned into the receiver as he pushed the release catch on the microwave and removed a shop-bought lasagne. Steam burned his thumb. "For God's sake!" Times like this, he missed his wife more than ever.

"It's me," Shania said, her voice shaky. "I'd like to talk."

Surprised, he paused mid-way through peeling back plastic on the carton. "All right, where?" Grabbing a pen from the odds-and-sods drawer, he flipped open a notepad at the end of the counter.

"Not the Last Drop... Somewhere I rarely go."

The DI thought about it. "What about The White Hart?"

There was a moment's silence. "Aye, all right... The White Hart."

"When?"

"In an hour?"

He checked his watch. In an hour, it would be eight-thirty. He was due to ring Jane at nine. "Yes, okay... See you there at eight-thirty." He would have to ring his wife earlier and explain. Perhaps Craig would still be up then, anyway, and he could have a quick chat with his eldest before speaking with his wife. He missed them all so much. The place wasn't home without his family. The two youngest children would have been in bed by the time he got home at seven-fifteen.

THE WHITE HART, a stone's throw from the Royal Mile, was an old establishment adorned with dark oak beams, low ceilings, and worn leather seats. A fiddler played in the corner while a few of the patrons watched and chatted.

When Shania walked into the pub fifteen minutes late, McKenzie was sitting in a corner, feeling less lonely than before, with a half-empty pint of ale in front of him. He looked up as she approached, eyes narrowing as he wondered why she wanted to meet. Was she finally going to talk?

They exchanged pleasantries, but with an underlying tension. The DI had the feeling he was being set up. His eyes flicked to the door and back.

Shania had dressed in a short denim skirt and yellow wool top, not quite long enough to cover her mid-riff. Her ears sported large metal hoops, and she smelled of cheap perfume. Despite the attempt to hide her nervousness with a smile, tight lips betrayed her. She leaned towards him, her voice low and seductive. "You know, DI McKenzie, I've always found a man in uniform intriguing."

"I'm not in uniform." He pulled a face.

She leaned back, crossing her long legs; lingering the motion.

McKenzie's gaze flicked to the legs and back, his expression unreadable. "Cut the act, Shania. I know this isn't you. Did they tell you to seduce me? Or are you ready to dish the dirt on the gang, and who is running it? And do you want a drink?"

"White wine." She pouted. "Was I that obvious?"

"Aye, you were." He left for the bar, returning minutes later with a glass of house white.

"So, what do we do now?"

"You start talking... Tell me what you know. Where is my nephew Gordon?"

Shania's smile faltered. She took a deep breath. "I don't know."

"Is that true? Or you are too scared to tell me?"

"Both."

"Do you know where he is?"

"No." She frowned at the disbelief on his face. "Honest... I don't know where he is. They wouldn't tell me, anyway. They would consider it too great a risk."

"But they have him, right?"

She shrugged. "I think so."

"Who has Gordon, Shania?"

She closed her mouth.

"Could you live with yourself if he ended up like Anderson?"

Her eyes widened, and she swallowed hard.

"Were you there when they hurt Mark?"

"No."

"But they killed him?"

"That is the rumour."

"Who murdered him?" McKenzie's eyes bored into hers.

Shania's fingers nervously traced the rim of her almost empty glass. "I can't say. If I tell you, you might as well add me to the list of victims now."

McKenzie leaned in, his voice low. "Shania, I can't protect you if I don't know who we are fighting."

Shania stared into her glass. "I can't risk it. They're watching... Always watching."

He cast his eyes around the White Hart. "Are any of them in here?"

She shook her head.

"Well, that's something..."

She pulled a blonde wig from her bag. "I wore this and left the back way. I told them I was in bed with a migraine."

"Would they have followed you otherwise?"

"Probably."

"Was that Anderson's job?"

She shifted position, eyes flicking to his face. "What do you mean?"

"Was he assigned to watch you? Like a guard? Or a chaperone?"

Her gaze dropped to the glass once more. For the first time in the conversation, McKenzie saw her eyes glisten with tears.

"He was watching you, wasn't he? So, who guards you now? And what about the other girls? Do they also have watchers?"

She neither denied nor confirmed his assertions.

"Do the names Kenny Doyle or Shaun McNeil mean anything to you?"

Her eyes were back on his. "No," she denied. "Why would they?"

"We found both their names and yours in the back of Mark Anderson's notebook."

She rose from her seat.

"What's the matter?"

"I have to go."

"Is it one of them? Or both? Who is running the show, Shania?"

The woman didn't reply. Having emptied her glass and grabbed her bag, she was already half-way through the door.

GORDON SAT HUNCHED, *alone, and shivering in the tunnel. He had perched his feet and bottom on either side of a thin stream of water snaking its route through the concrete pipe. It was the only way to keep them dry. But, when he slept, he invariably woke to find one part or other soaked. The blanket around his shoulders felt damp and cold where he leaned against the tunnel wall. It was impossible to find a comfortable position.*

He'd given up crying about his situation. And he had cried. On and off for three days straight. He no longer knew how long he had been in that hole. Though they had brought food, it was never enough, always cold, and barely edible. One day they had forgotten to bring him any at all, and he had resorted to wetting his lips with the cruddy water trickling along the bottom of the pipe.

He thought of his mother, and the distress she would be in, feeling guilt at the way he had sometimes taken her for granted. Goose would have done anything to be at home with her now, smelling her cooking and giving her a hug. He wondered if he would ever see his parents and sister Mona again, but pushed those thoughts away, as he had done many times since they had taken him.

Gordon had been sure they would kill him when they bagged his head and dragged him into the back of a car. He was grateful to be alive, but confused about what was going on. Was he being ransomed? His middle-class parents wouldn't have that much in the bank. Had he offended someone? If so, who? How?

Footsteps echoing off the damp concrete walls shattered the oppressive silence in the tunnel. Gordon's heart thumped as he huddled deeper into his wet cover, eyes wide.

Two figures emerged from the shadows, one taller and more imposing than the other. The larger man, with a hard face and scar on his temple, motioned to his pal. "Grab his arm," he ordered.

Gordon opened his mouth to protest, though he didn't know what was happening. Was he being freed? Or something worse? He clamped his jaws shut.

The second man, a stocky individual with large biceps, approached Gordon with a sneer, pulling him roughly to his feet. Goose stumbled, gasping in pain. His body ached from the long period of confinement, but he had learned to endure his discomfort in silence. He bit his lip.

They dragged him through the tunnel, his feet scraping against the wet concrete floor. Goose gathered his thoughts. If he was going to escape, he had to be ready for the least opportunity. But, perhaps this time, he would find out why they had taken him.

Once inside the lair, the henchmen forced Gordon into a rickety wooden chair. Cold, unyielding metal handcuffs bit into his wrists.

The first man took a seat across from him, eyes cold and calculating.

"So, Goose," he sneered, "I've heard interesting things about your uncle, DI McKenzie." He leaned forward, his breath rancid like sour milk. "How far would he be willing to go to save your ass, do you think? Shall we put it to the test?"

Gordon shook his head. "No..."

"His family is not at home. I wonder why?" The tormentor

sniggered before leaning closer to Gordon's sweating face. *"Where would they have gone?"*

"I don't know what you mean..." Goose coughed, a dry, hoarse hack.

"Don't mess me about..." The man pushed Gordon's head back. *"I mean his wife and kids. Where are they?"*

"How would I know?"

The interrogator slapped his face. *"Where would they go? Where would they consider safe?"*

"I don't know."

"Stop messing me about," he growled, grabbing Gordon by the hair, pulling his head back. *"Take a wild guess..."*

Goose's mind raced. His uncle had always been a source of pride and protection for him as a child. He had no wish to sell either Grant or his family down river. *"I do not know where they would go,"* he replied, his voice quivering.

The man leaned in closer, his massive frame cast a menacing shadow over the quaking lad. He raised a fist, ready to throw a punch. Goose flinched, bracing for impact, but his persecutor paused, exhaling loudly through his nostrils. *"You can make this easy or you can make it hard."*

"Why are you doing this?" Gordon blurted. *"I have done nothing to you..."*

"Except chase one of our girls, eh? What? Do you think she would be interested in you? Shania likes your uncle." His grin was a vicious snarl.

Goose lifted wide eyes to his tormentor.

"Aye, that's right... They went out for a drink last night. What do you think about that? And you thought he was a family man? I bet you don't know the half of it... So why do you want to protect him? What's he doing for you, eh? Apart from chasing your fancy woman? Why hasn't he been here to rescue you? Where's the cavalry? Let me help you out... They're not coming.

He can't chase Shania with you in the way. Think about it. You should be more careful where you place your loyalty."

Gordon shook his head, his hair clinging to him from sweat. "He's not like that. He's not like you," he spat in defiance.

It garnered another slap from the thug; the sound echoing around the room. "Bring the water, lads..."

22

A PERILOUS JOURNEY

"**A**re going to tell us now?" They lifted his head out of the water.

Gordon gasped for air, shaking his head; sending droplets flying around him.

"More!" The thug ordered. "He's not using his brains today."

"No, please-" Goose's head went back under the water, bubbles gurgling to the surface as he threshed and strained against those holding him.

Once more, they lifted him out by the hair. "Well, where is your uncle's family?"

Goose spat and snorted water while he thought about his cousins. All three were so young. How could he give them away to these monsters? He was desperate to get out of the situation. Each time they held him under, he thought he would die. But the children were so young, and his Aunt Jane had always been kind to him. He couldn't be the one to let them down. He couldn't. Gordon knew he would never forgive himself if they were harmed. And he loved his uncle Grant. He bit his tongue.

The man held up his hand. "Stop... If he won't talk, we have no alternative. Take him to the hill."

Goose gasped and gulped air, water dripping from every part of him. His shirt was soaked, and he shivered in the light from the lamps. What did they mean, take him to the hill?

"Fine... Don't say I didn't warn you," the brute growled, waving his hand dismissively. "You have no-one to blame but yourself. Take him away."

~

KENNY DOYLE LOCKED the office door at The Eclipse nightclub, checking his watch. He would have to leave immediately if he was to get there on time. He had a reputation for punctuality, and this one he did not want to miss.

He placed the signature baseball cap on his head and set off down the close to where he had left his car.

~

AT FAIRWAY HAVEN, Shaun McNeil slid on his harlequin jacket. He didn't need his driver for this mission. Grabbing the keys to the Porsche, he slipped out, checking his watch. He would be there in plenty of time for the finale.

~

"YOU KNOW we took Mark Anderson up there, don't you?" The taller of the two henchmen sneered as the car sped along. He sat on one side of Goose, and the stocky gorilla sat on the other.

In front, the driver had his back to them and did not look round.

"What?" Gordon frowned. "What do you mean?"

"Oh, of course... You wouldn't know... You spent your time in a concrete pipe."

"*Do you mean Mark Anderson from Corstophine?*"

"*Aye, that would be the one.*"

"*What do you mean, you took him up there? Do you mean up to Arthur's Seat?*" he asked, looking through the window.

"*Anderson did not know where we were going, or why.*"

"*What did you do to him?*" Goose asked, though he might easily guess the answer.

"*Have you got that copy of the paper?*" The lanky henchman asked of the broad one.

"*Not with me,*" was the grunted reply.

Gordon swallowed hard. "*I don't like this... Why don't you let me go? It'll be easier for you, if you do.*"

"*Easier, how?*" The tall man frowned. "*No-one is gonna know we brought you up here. Look... No cameras.*" He held his hands up, swinging them towards the windows.

"*What happened to Mark?*"

"*Let's just say that beggar breathes no more.*"

"*You killed him?*"

"*He's bright this one, eh?*" the stocky guy said. "*No flies on him...*"

"*You'll go away from a long time,*" Goose said, defiantly. "*My uncle will have you behind bars faster than you can shit.*"

"*The kid has a mouth.*" The first henchman sneered. "*Make the most of it. It'll soon be closed... permanently.*"

23

CHASE BEHIND RICHMOND STREET

S hania ran into the station at Leith, panting as she reached the front desk. "I'd like…" She bent over, holding her sides while she regained enough breath to talk. "I'd like to speak with DI McKenzie, please?" she finally managed.

"Can I tell him what it's about?" Stuart, the civilian manning the desk, asked. He dialled the number for the MIT.

"Tell him it's Shania." She hitched her bag up on her shoulder. "He'll surely want to see me."

Stuart raised a brow, punching in McKenzie's extension. "Sir, there's a Shania here asking to see you?"

"She's in the station?"

"Aye, she's here waiting for you."

"Tell her I'll be right there."

~

GRANT TOOK the stairs two at a time down to reception. He didn't know what had brought Shania to the station, but it had to be important.

He nodded a thank you to Stuart and gestured for the young woman to follow him to an interview room.

She wiped her palms on her skirt as they entered the small room and took a seat before being asked.

McKenzie closed the door behind them, sitting across from her. He leaned forward, concern etched on his face. "All right, Shania, what's this all about? Why the urgency?"

The girl glanced around the room, her eyes scanning for cameras or microphones. "Is this private?"

"Nothing from in here will go to anyone it shouldn't, if that is worrying you?"

She frowned. "How can you be sure?"

"What's this about? I can't help you if you won't tell me anything."

"It's about your nephew..."

The DI's eyes widened, and he leaned in, his expression grave. "Gordon? What about him? What do you know?"

She glanced behind at the door, satisfying herself there was no-one there.

"Shania... What's happened to him?"

She swallowed hard, her voice trembling. "He's in danger. They've taken him somewhere. I don't know where. Apparently, they were holding him in some old concrete tunnels, and they've moved him."

"How do you know this?"

"I got it out of Jock Munro."

McKenzie's jaw tightened as he absorbed the information. "Why would Jock know where they're keeping my nephew?"

Shania hesitated for a moment, choosing her words carefully. "He is my new watcher, and he's working for with the gang. Jock's been with them for a while... Since before they took Gordon. I didn't know him that well, then. But, since Mark was... Well, they have assigned him to me. We wouldn't normally get friendly with the men who watch us. But I knew if anyone could find out where your nephew was, it would be Munro. He's not as loyal to Gordon as everyone thinks he is. I think he gave the gang the information that led to Goose being taken in the first place."

The DI ran a hand through his hair. "Do you have any idea where Jock might be right now?"

She shook her head.

"Who's running this gang, Shania? Who is the power behind this shit show? Is it Doyle? McNeil?"

She chewed her bottom lip. "I don't know his identity. I've never met him outside of the organisation, and only know him as The Man. It's how he makes everyone refer to him. They must never refer to him by name. He hides behind the fake companies that launder his money. If you go after him, you have to take him down. He'll think nothing of killing you and everyone you love. I only know that he trusts his male employees more than the girls. He rates them highly. If anyone will know, it's Munro."

McKenzie nodded. "We'll handle it from here, Shania. Thank you for coming forward. Is there somewhere safe you can go? We have a witness protection programme. You could get away from this gang."

"When this is over, I'll be going to my mother's. She has a croft in the Shetlands. It's pretty remote."

"Do you have money?"

"I've saved what I need. It'll buy me some time, at least until I know what I want to do with my future. I might even go to university, eh?"

"Well, you can stay here at the station for as long as you

need to. Let me know if you require our help to get to your mother's."

"My stepdad will pick me up... The gang thinks my parents live in Glasgow. I've never told them the truth. I always knew there'd come a time when I would want to escape their clutches. And I always worried they would try forcing me to stay. They never let their top earners go."

McKenzie checked his watch. "Speaking of which, I'd better get on. God only knows what the gang intend doing with my nephew. I'll send DC Helen McAllister down. She will take a statement from you and help you organise your move."

"Don't mention my name to anyone in that gang, and not to Munro." Shania frowned. "I don't want them knowing I said anything."

Grant nodded before leaving the room.

"Oh no, you don't!" McKenzie set off, running down the close behind Richmond Street. "Jock, stop!" he shouted, fighting with a sheet that swung at him behind the fleeing Munro.

The DI had received intel that Jock was at the Elite-Fusion Gym, and had gone there to question him. Unfortunately for Grant, Munro had seen him from a window high above the backstreet, and fled, still wearing his gym gear.

McKenzie's heart pounded as he chased after the lad, cursing because his leather shoes were no match for the trainers his quarry was wearing. He followed the lad through the narrow close behind Richmond, his breath coming in gasps as he closed the distance between them. "Stop... Jock, I only want to talk to you..."

Distant sounds from the city became muffled in the confined space of the close. As he closed in on Munro, McKenzie's frustration increased. Jock held vital information about his nephew. Goose's life was at stake, and this lad was supposed to be his best friend. He should have had his back. But Jock had been the traitor who had put the safety of sister's son, and the DI's own family, at risk. "You won't get away, you might as well give up!" McKenzie's fierce tone sliced through the quiet ambience between the rows of houses. He lunged forward, grabbing a post in his path and using it to propel himself.

Jock was running out of steam.

Finally, the DI closed the gap. He reached out, panting hard; strong fingers curling around the collar of Jock's gym shirt. With a surge of irritation and determination, he yanked the lad backward, causing him to stumble and crash into a gable wall at the end of the street.

Breathing heavily, McKenzie pinned Jock against the cold stone wall. His face inches from the lad; eyes burning with intense anger. "You're not going anywhere until you tell me where they've taken Gordon."

Munro's own eyes were wide as he stammered in response. "M- Mr McKenzie, you don't understand... They forced me to tell them about Gordon. They heard you were a big fish in MIT, and that you had a nephew in my circle of friends. I had no choice, I swear. They threatened to hurt me and my family if I didn't set up the snatch. I'm worried about him, too... I swear to God... I am scared for him, just like you are."

McKenzie's grip on Munro's collar loosened, though he still held onto him, searching Jock's eyes for signs of deceit. The tension in the alley was palpable, with the fate of Gordon hanging in the balance. "So, where is he?" The DI's thunderous expression told the lad he would brook no nonsense.

"Arthur's Seat," Jock blurted, his voice trembling. "They're taking Gordon up to Arthur's Seat."

"Why there?"

Jock swallowed hard, his gaze dropping to the ground. "They said it's a message to you, and to Shania. They want everyone to see what happens to those who cross them. Goose is in danger. I didn't want any of this to happen. I swear I didn't."

"Who runs the show, Jock? Is it McNeil? The guy who runs the golf and gambling resorts? Does he own this gym? Is that why you went there?"

"I don't know, I swear. We refer to the leader only as The Man. I've only ever spoken with people who work for him. And no-one dares speak his name."

"Don't lie to me."

"I'm not. His face is always in darkness. He shines bright light on our faces to hide his identity. I can't be sure who he is."

McKenzie let go his grip on Jock's collar as he processed the information. Once again, the ancient and extinct volcano looming over Edinburgh was to be a place of execution. "Not on my watch," he said aloud.

"What do we do now?" Munro asked, relieved the DI had released his grip.

"Present yourself at Leith station. I'll tell them to expect you." McKenzie said, his tone softer, but no less determined.

"Am I under arrest?"

"I haven't decided yet. You have critical information. If you talk, it will be easier on you. It could reduce the number of charges you face."

Grant called the DCI on his mobile.

24

PERIL ON ARTHUR'S SEAT

"McKenzie?" DCI Sinclair sounded surprised at the call from Grant.

"I need an armed response team, dogs; the complete works, up at Arthur's Seat as soon as possible."

"What's going on?"

The DI could almost hear Sinclair's frown on the other end of the line. "Gang members are taking my nephew Gordon up there to make an example of him."

"Christ!"

Seconds passed. McKenzie could hear heavy breathing on the other end. "Sir?"

"All right, I'll sort it. What are you going to do?"

"I'm heading up there. Tell the teams no sirens. If the gang gets wind of us, they'll kill my nephew."

"Understood."

"Tell them no helicopters unless I call for one. I don't want them spooked. Stealth is required."

The DCI cleared his throat. "Don't try doing anything before your backup arrives, unless Gordon's life really is in danger."

"Understood."

"Go canny."

"I will."

～

THE MAN PUNCHED Gordon hard to the stomach.

Retching and groaning in pain, Goose fell to his knees.

The kingpin's henchmen held the sagging, injured lad up by his arms while their leader punched him again, this time to the head.

Gordon spat blood. Teeth loosened by the blow, wobbled against his tongue. He braced himself for the next onslaught.

"Shaun McNeil!" Grant's voice growled from behind the group as he approached over the grass, his expression as moody as the thunderous clouds gathering overhead. "Stand back! You're surrounded by armed police."

McNeil stopped mid-punch, swinging round to witness the bearer of the booming voice. "Where? I don't see any officers."

"Grant..." Goose mumbled, his eyes lighting up; sweat dripping from his forehead.

"So, this is your famous uncle, eh? The great DI McKenzie?" The crime lord turned towards the detective. "You better stay where you are or we'll finish him."

Grant waited, a violent thudding in his chest. He longed to rip out McNeil's heart with his bare hands. But he stood, teeth and fists clenched; chin jutting in the wind. "You'll see my colleagues soon enough."

"If you value your family, you'll not stand in our way... They'll not be safe if I end up in jail. They'll not be safe anywhere."

"Is that what you tell the girls? All the women you

coerce into performing for your financial gain? Bullies like you never prosper. You might get rich in the short-term but, in the long run, you'll rot behind bars, which is where you belong. Now, let Gordon go."

"Who? This Gordon?" McNeil punched McKenzie's nephew again.

Grant took a step forward, his face contorted with pained anxiety for the young man who hung, groaning, from the henchmen's grip. "You bastard!" The DI spat the words, every muscle in his body taught.

"Aye, well, you can call me names if you like... But I hold all the cards, eh? Take another step, and your precious nephew will only be good as food for thistles."

The taller of the two henchmen took a handgun from his pocket; placing the muzzle to Goose's temple.

As McKenzie's body trembled with repressed fear and anger at the plight of Gordon, he heard vehicle tyres on the gravel below. Van and car doors opened and closed. He knew that sound. Help was close. "I'll ask you again to release Gordon, and step back. You can't leave here. There is nowhere for you to go. Anything you do now will only make it worse for you later."

McNeil grabbed the gun from his grunt and aimed it at the DI. "Nothing I can do, eh? What about I shoot you dead right here? What about that?"

"How old are you, McNeil? Fifties? Armed police are moving up the hill as we speak. Shoot me, and they'll guarantee you never see daylight again. You're already responsible for Mark Anderson's death; probably Sheryl O'Farrell's, too. And we will prove it. Add another scalp, and they'll throw away the key."

Armed officers fanned out over the grass. "Drop your

weapon and put your hands above your head!" they ordered.

Behind him, Grant could hear the Alsatians barking, eager to be loosed from their leashes.

McNeil heard them too. He glanced at his men as they let Goose fall to the ground. All three took several paces back before fleeing off to McKenzie's right.

Shots rang out. McNeil tumbled to the ground. His men stopped in their tracks, hands in the air. "Don't shoot!" the stocky one begged.

Their leader rolled around on the floor, moaning and holding his right thigh to stem the blood. His gun lay loose in the grass.

McKenzie ran to his nephew, helping him to his feet before holding the shivering lad. Hands either side of Goose's head, the DI scoured the young man's face. "Are you okay, Gordon?"

Elation overcoming pain, the boy nodded. "I am now. I thought I was a goner."

McKenzie's face darkened; his expression, grim. "You very nearly were."

"I don't know why any of this happened." Goose grimaced, his body still shaking. "What did I do wrong?"

Grant shook his head. "You did nothing wrong, Gordon. None of this was your fault. I'll explain once we have you safe and those low-lives in custody."

KENNY DOYLE HUGGED his fourteen-year-old son, Stuart, in celebration of Celtic's goal against Rangers. They jumped up and down, screaming at the top of their lungs, "Come on! We got this!" at the equaliser, shaking and pumping their fists in the air. The boys in the green and white stripes jumped all over each other on the pitch before running back to their positions. There was still work to do.

This time with his lad was precious, and had been since Doyle and the boy's mother estranged from each other six years before.

"We can do this." Kenny hugged his lad again. "Ten minutes to go, and one-all. The momentum is with us now. Keep it up lads," he shouted, his voice ringing out with all the others willing on their team. "Keep it going. Pile on the pressure." Only ten minutes before, their end of the stadium had been steeped in gloom as they stared potential defeat in the face. It was serious stuff, this rivalry between the foremost football teams in Scotland. Known together as 'The Old Firm,' both hailed from Glasgow and had dominated the Scottish football scene for the best part of a hundred years. These games were equivalent to life or death in the minds of their most avid fans. Some would say the rivalry had contributed to sectarian and religious tensions in Scotland; others simply enjoyed the enduring bitter competition between the two camps that made the wins so much sweeter and the losses nigh-on unbearable.

Today, however, there was to be the satisfaction of neither team. They settled for a one-all draw.

A deflated Kenny and son wandered to the nearest pub for a consolation stout and bitter-shandy. There would be no singing at the top of their voices today.

25

DAY AFTER THE MONTH BEFORE

Paramedics rushed forward to take charge of Gordon, as uniformed officers arrested a still-moaning McNeil and his two grunts. They carried away the crime lord in handcuffs on a stretcher towards a waiting ambulance, accompanied by two heavily armed officers. They marched his men to the nearest police van and placed them in the cage at the back.

McKenzie gave his nephew's shoulder a squeeze. "I'll leave you in these guys' capable hands," he said of the paramedics. "I'll talk to your mum. She'll be over the moon..."

"Aye..." Goose nodded. "Tell her I'm sorry..."

"For what?" McKenzie pushed his hands deep into his overcoat pockets. "For getting yourself kidnapped? You did nothing wrong. She and your dad will be ecstatic you're safe. They'll not be worrying about anything else."

"What about Shania?" Gordon's eyes narrowed as he wiped at the blood around his mouth, remembering the words of McNeil when he told him his uncle had been after her.

"She's in a safe place. You might contact her further down the road when that lot gets the jail sentences they deserve. I think she likes you," he added.

"Really?" Goose's face lit up.

"Aye, but you'll need to be patient a wee while. Promise you won't try to find her before then?"

"Aye, I promise."

"Good. We'll let her know you were asking for her."

"And Jock?"

McKenzie grimaced. "We'll need to have a conversation about your mate when you're feeling better."

Gordon frowned. "Wait, was he involved in what happened to me?"

"To an extent..." Grant nodded. "I think he's sorry now. He got involved with the McNeil gang and ended up in deep water. The lad is regretting it now, but he's got a long way to go before he has made amends. He'll probably get a community sentence." McKenzie checked his watch. "Anyway, I'll leave these guys to it and catch up with you later. I'll go find your mother."

DAVINA, in sweatpants and a tee shirt, wrenched open the door before McKenzie was half-way down the garden path. "Where is he?" she asked, eyes wide; face glowing.

"News travels fast." Her brother grinned as she grabbed him by the arms.

"It's been all over the telly. They are still reporting from up on Arthur's Seat. Is he okay?"

Her brother nodded. "As he can be, given what he's been through. They've taken him to the Western General to check him over," he said, referring to the large hospital in Edinburgh.

"Can we see him?"

"I don't see why not. They may let him go tonight once they've given him the okay."

"Och, I canna wait that long." Davina tossed her head. "I'll phone Jim; see if he can knock off early. Otherwise, I'll get a taxi."

Grant pulled a face. "I'd give you a lift, except I better get back to the station."

"Aye, no worries. You get back." Davina gave him a hug. "And thank you. I knew you'd get him back to us."

DC Graham Dalgleish socketed the phone on his desk as McKenzie walked through the door back at Leith Station. "Och, there he is..." He grinned. "You were playing hooky again?"

"Am I in trouble?" Grant grimaced.

"I don't know. He's not been through yet," Graham replied, referring to DCI Sinclair. "When I looked through his window, he was on the phone. And congratulations, by the way."

"I had to tell him... I needed backup."

"Och, he'll be fine. He might have a go at you, but I don't think he'll do anything drastic. You'll not face disciplinary. I can't see him doing that."

Grant nodded. "Gordon's safe. That is the main thing. I'll face whatever Sinclair throws my way. It was worth it."

"Aye, and McNeil is headed where he belongs."

DS Susan Robertson came through the door. "The wanderer returns." She grinned, handing McKenzie a mug of tea. "You deserve that."

"Where's mine?" Dalgleish pulled a face.

"You can make your own. You haven't been chasing violent thugs around Arthur's Seat."

"Aye, fair enough."

McKenzie laughed. "You two are like a bickering couple. When's the divorce?"

"What was that?" Susan asked. "You don't want the hot drink, you say? I can have it myself? Och, that's very nice of you."

Grant pulled the mug to his chest. "Don't. I need it, thank you."

DC Helen McAllister walked into the room, her face solemn. "They've confessed to the murder of Sheryl O'Farrell and given us a location for her body."

Grant plopped his mug on the desk. "Where?"

"You will not like it." She shook her head.

Grant's eyes narrowed. "What did they do with her?"

"They cut her up after she was dead and divided the parts between multiple bins within the city. If they are telling us the truth, she ended up in landfill."

McKenzie closed his eyes. Searching landfill was a hell of a job, and it was nigh-on impossible to find a whole person in there, let alone a body in bits. It wasn't the news he wanted to give to her family. "Damn it!" He ran both hands through his hair.

"I'm sorry, Grant. I know you wanted to find her for the relatives."

"She deserves to rest in peace," he answered.

"Forensics will do their best..."

"Aye... I know."

"There is good news, however."

"Thank God." McKenzie sipped his brew.

"Shania has gone to her mother's croft. She's planning on taking online courses, and seems determined to better her future."

"Well, that is great news." The DI checked his watch. "I'd better go. Jane and the children will be on their way home. I've missed them so much."

"Aye, you go." Dalgleish nodded. "I'll speak to Sinclair; smooth things over."

"Thanks, Graham." McKenzie squeezed the DC's shoulder. "I owe you."

McKENZIE RESISTED the urge to run the length of his garden path until the last four pavers. Rain had rendered them sleek and his shoes sorely needed replacing, but with the last few metres to go, he raced to the front door, wrenching the keys from his pocket.

Before he had time to get one in the lock, Jane had opened it; wee Martha clinging on to her arm. "Grant..."

He knew that smile. The one that said she'd missed him. The one that echoed everything he had felt since the last time he had seen his family.

They held onto each other for several minutes, joined by Craig and Davie.

"Group hug." Jane nuzzled her face in his chest.

"We missed you so much, dad," Davie said.

"Aye lad, and you cannot imagine how much I missed you... All of you. Don't be leaving like that again."

His wife pulled her head back from his shirt front to look into his eyes. "We won't."

The End

Printed in Great Britain
by Amazon

39808821R00101